She wanted t... the secret ma...

Lukas disappeared between the dusty stone walls as Nadia watched him go fill the water bottle, his limber strides covering the ground with a smooth economy of effort. Briefly she closed her eyes. She hated deceiving him, but she just couldn't be sure he wasn't deceiving her. Besides, she wanted to follow the map the old woman had given her, see what the *X* on it meant.

She got up restlessly, stepping out of the shelter of the willow boughs. Should she try to give him the slip? *Could* she?

A bird broke off in midnote, and a faint sound brought Nadia's glance up. The scream in her throat was caught stillborn.

From the roof of the vacant house a heavy clay tile hurtled down toward her head....

ABOUT THE AUTHOR

Tina Vasilos has successfully written romantic suspense for a number of years. Widely traveled, she knows Greece thoroughly, having married a Greek some seventeen years ago and gone to explore it many times. She and her husband live with their teenage son in Clearbrook, British Columbia, where they've been since 1979.

Books by Tina Vasilos

HARLEQUIN INTRIGUE

68–UNWITTING ACCOMPLICE

Wolf's Prey

Tina Vasilos

Harlequin Books

TORONTO • NEW YORK • LONDON
AMSTERDAM • PARIS • SYDNEY • HAMBURG
STOCKHOLM • ATHENS • TOKYO • MILAN

To John, with all my love.
I couldn't have done it without you.

Harlequin Intrigue edition published November 1988

ISBN 0-373-22101-0

Printed in U.S.A.

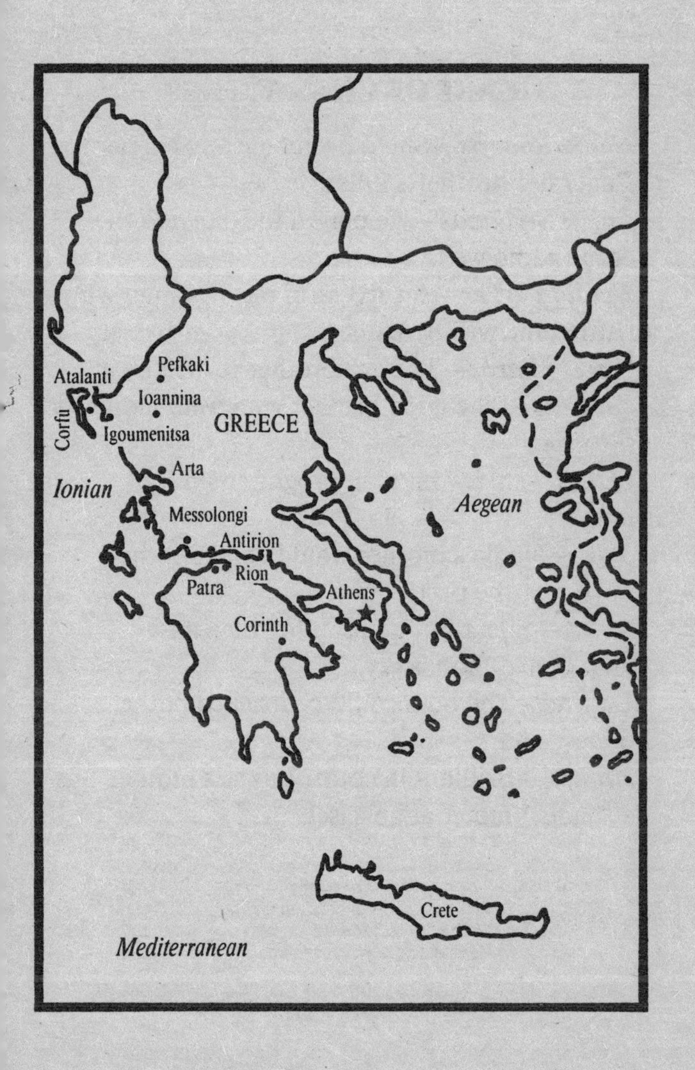
Pefkaki
Atalanti
Ioannina
GREECE
Corfu
Igoumenitsa
Arta
Ionian
Messolongi
Antirion
Rion
Patra
Athens
Corinth
Aegean
Crete
Mediterranean

CAST OF CHARACTERS

Nadia Roberts—She'd overcome any barrier to finger her brother's killer.

Lukas Stylianos—He played the lute *and* the crime game well.

Gerald Parker—A successful businessman who ruffled the wrong feathers.

Angelo Paros—The evil brother reviled by all.

Andreas—The good brother who went along for the ride.

Halias—An icy hit man programmed for murder.

Sally—Nadia's mother would confront the horror of the past.

Monk—Silent but helpful, he ruled an abandoned monastery.

Gabriel—The boss could be reached at the oddest hours.

Anthea—Brilliant in court, Lukas's mother was a shade dimmer at an easel.

Chapter One

Pulling a tissue from her tote bag, Nadia Roberts wiped perspiration from her face. Although a brisk sea wind had pulled at her hair as she crossed the airport tarmac, she found the car hot inside, much hotter than she was used to in April.

Dust and exhaust fumes drifted into the open windows. Bricks and rubble lined the broad avenue leading from the Athens airport to the city center, turning it into a scene of chaos.

The six lanes of traffic were at a standstill, impatient drivers leaning on their horns as if sheer noise might get them moving again.

The man beside her tapped his fingers on the steering wheel, lips pursed as he whistled softly in time to the music that was coming from a tape deck mounted beneath the dash of the little car. The music was strange to Nadia's ears, an almost Oriental dissonance underlying the strong notes of a clarinet and the plaintive voice of a singer wailing about lost love or invasion or some other catastrophe.

"What's holding up the traffic?" Nadia spoke abruptly, glancing at the man, who returned her gaze with unmistakable amusement in his amber cat's eyes.

"It's often like this." His voice was deep, his English fluent, spoken with an almost British inflection that fell pleasantly on her ears. Although he hadn't said or done much beyond introducing himself and helping her retrieve her luggage, she had noticed the idioms he used freely, his precise accent endowing commonplace phrases with an exotic unfamiliarity.

Lukas Stylianos was his name. He was a Greek policeman. Assigned to investigate her brother's death, which had occurred less than a week ago.

"Please accept my sympathy," he had said quietly when she climbed into the tiny Renault. With complete self-confidence, he sent the car roaring out of the parking lot, then skirted past a more sedate Mercedes onto the highway.

A monstrous traffic jam took over about halfway to the city. They'd been sitting now for the better part of an hour. "The road is being rebuilt to make it more efficient, but who knows when it will be complete," Lukas added, putting the car into gear as the vehicle ahead inched forward.

A white-gloved traffic policeman directed them around a large crater in the next intersection. The flourishing gestures of his hands gave him the look of an orchestra conductor.

"At last," Nadia muttered as the car accelerated down the palm-lined boulevard.

Lukas glanced at her. "One thing you'd better be aware of at the outset is that nothing is like what you're used to. Some things are accomplished more slowly, others faster than in Vancouver. Greeks are great believers in priorities, but the priorities tend to differ from those in North America."

"Finding out the circumstances around my brother's death can't wait," she said, her voice breaking despite her effort to control it. The past week had been the worst of her life. She had only just received a cheerful letter from Gerald, saying he was going to the area north of Ioannina on business. Then the very next day she had gotten the news. He was dead.

She straightened in her seat, adjusting the seat belt to a more comfortable angle across her chest. "Gerald was not the kind of man who had enemies. I'd like to find out who killed him, and why."

"Don't worry, Nadia—I can call you Nadia, can't I?"

She lifted one shoulder and let it drop. "What's the difference?"

"Nadia, all of us would like to find out what happened to your brother. Don't act as if I'm here to block your path."

"Aren't you?" she countered. "Isn't it tempting just to sweep the whole affair under the rug? 'Canadian has unfortunate accident in remote Greek village.' Done and forgotten, especially when the victim was not particularly welcome."

"When a man is beaten and then shot in the head, it cannot be dismissed as an unfortunate accident." His voice was harsh.

Nadia closed her eyes, remembering the horror of receiving that phone call. His body had been found in the mountains of northwestern Greece. Fortunately he'd listed her on his passport as next of kin. As a result, she'd been able to break the news gently to their parents.

Tears stung her eyes, a mixture of sorrow and anger at the senselessness and violence of his death. Murder. Although they had decided to follow Gerald's wish that he be buried in the country where he had spent so much time these past ten years, she couldn't help but regret having had to miss the funeral. By the time they'd received the news, it had been too late; friends of Gerry's from Athens had had to suffice. They'd gone up to Epirus and seen to the arrangements.

That might have been the end of the matter—except for the autopsy report. She knew all the cold facts detailing the cause of death, including the horrifying statement that he had been identified mainly through papers found in his pockets. She had listened to the assurances of consulate staff that everything possible would be done to find and convict Gerald's killer. Because of his Greek birth, the investigation was to be conducted by Greek police.

Nadia had been dissatisfied with their politely worded platitudes. She had come here to see that the right questions were asked, the strongest possible investigation conducted. She wanted to see that the killer was punished.

They had assigned Lukas Stylianos to help her. She was convinced he'd been selected as her personal watchdog.

"We rely on the tourist industry," Lukas was saying. "It's suffered enough damage in the past several years from world terrorism that we can't afford any more international incidents. Rest assured that we're doing all we can.''

He sounded sincere, she had to give him that. And he looked intelligent. He brought the car to a screeching halt at a changing traffic light, and she opened her eyes. As he concentrated on the sea of noisy, exhaust-belching vehicles that hemmed them in, she studied him.

He was handsome, although not classically so. His face was too lean, too dark, an arresting composition of hard planes and incisive lines of character. His nose was strong, aquiline, his eyes hazel, clear and glowing, framed by thick black lashes.

He caught her staring, and smiled before depressing the clutch and shifting into first, missing her blush as he sent the car snarling across the intersection.

Nadia forcibly reined in her errant thoughts. ''Mr. Stylianos—''

''Lukas,'' he interrupted.

She nodded. Formality was pointless, she knew, since it was obvious she was stuck with him. ''Lukas, can you tell me what's been done so far?''

''Not much.'' He put up a hand as she scowled darkly. ''Don't get upset, Nadia. Not enough time's elapsed, and because of the international overtones of the case, village police were held at bay. Athens wants to direct it, so I was assigned as special investigator. I've handled this kind of case before. I was about to go up to Epirus when we heard you were coming. So here we are.''

''I have to check in with the Canadian Embassy,'' Nadia said. ''Could you take me there?''

Lukas glanced at his watch as he waited for yet another traffic light. "They're closed for the day now. You'll have to see them tomorrow morning."

"They tried to discourage me from accompanying the Athens police on an investigation." She lifted her chin. "But I came anyway."

He looked at her, his expression alert, waiting.

"I had to," she said with a determination that came from deep within her. "You don't object, do you?"

She thought she detected a glint of admiration in his extraordinary eyes. "I may have some misgivings, but no, we can't stop a foreigner accompanying us, when a family member's involved. It's your choice to put yourself in that sort of jeopardy."

On that she clenched her jaw once more, and hardly noticed when they screeched to a halt in front of her hotel.

LUKAS INHALED APPRECIATIVELY as he walked up the flagstone path around the house. Pristine white freesias scented the warm spring day, their poignant sweetness seeming to convey a quality of innocence that was foreign to his own life and work. He never forgot to be grateful that they had retained this house; it was only a half hour from the city center, yet on a quiet street far removed from the hurly-burly of modern Athens with its commerce and increasingly impersonal apartment buildings.

He let himself in by the back door, skirting bins of potatoes and sacks of beans on the porch. The house was quiet, but he knew his mother would be somewhere about. The thought brought an involuntary smile to his lips. Some of his friends ribbed him about living with his mother at the age of thirty-one, but despite their derisive comments he enjoyed her company, finding Anthea's astute observations on life and some of the cases he discussed with her stimulating and enlightening. She was an attorney, he was in law enforcement; the two fields were complementary.

He found her in her studio, reading glasses perched precariously on the end of her nose, the tip of a paintbrush between her teeth.

"Oh, hello, dear," she said absently, tilting her head this way and that as she studied the painting on the easel. "What do you think? A little more yellow in the tulips? Or is it too bright?"

Placing his hands on her shoulders, Lukas dropped a kiss onto her smooth cheek, breathing in the familiarity of the Balenciaga perfume she'd favored for years. "I think it's fine."

Pursing her lips, Anthea made a final dab at the lurid acrylic blob that was her impression of a spring flower, and dropped the brush into a convenient jar of water. She stood up, stretching her arms over her head as she flexed her back.

"Getting old and stiff," she muttered. "And that cold spell we had last week didn't help any."

Lukas threw an arm around her shoulders with easy affection. "You'll never be old, Mother."

It was true. The skin on a handsome, strong-boned face was soft, well cared for, and almost as unlined as a girl's. Tall, only a couple of inches shorter than Lukas's own height of six feet, she retained a slender form and erect carriage that belied her fifty-nine years.

Anthea came from a proud old family, and it showed in the intelligence that shone from her deep, warm brown eyes. Far from living off the achievements of her forebears, she had followed her father's advice and obtained an education. She had always worked, except for brief periods of time after the birth of each of her three children, and Lukas was proud of her, as his father had been.

Moving into the kitchen, Lukas placed cutlery and a salad retrieved from the refrigerator on the table, while Anthea dished up their lunch from a pot that had been simmering on the stove.

Lukas eyed the concoction of stewed artichokes, chick-peas and rice with a certain disfavor. "I thought you didn't consider fasting during Lent important," he grumbled mildly. "This year you seem to have outdone yourself. Fish and vegetables, vegetables, rice and fish, with an occasional break for bean soup."

"This is Holy Week," she reminded him. "Even the most lax of us show some reverence. I happen to know you went out to a restaurant last night. What did you have, chicken or lamb?"

"Barbecued pork," he replied without a trace of shame.

"And today you have this. A little deprivation is good for the soul."

"Good for the soul, maybe, but can my body stand it?" Sketching a perfunctory sign of the cross, he began to eat the Spartan food that, despite his complaints, was expertly prepared and surprisingly tasty.

His mother dipped a chunk of bread into the salad bowl and chewed it with relish. "This unfortunate business you're investigating has brought home to me that perhaps we're becoming too casual about our traditions. We'd better be careful, or someone will take them away from us. We're getting so complacent, they'd be gone before we were aware of theft."

"Not likely." Lukas got up to fetch a cold beer from the fridge and uncapped it. He downed half the bottle in one swallow. He reseated himself, attacking the chick-peas once more. "Still, I agree it's arrogant of someone to come in from outside and start interfering in local affairs. Did Gerald Parker really think he was going to get instant cooperation from the locals, simply by trying to teach them more efficient methods of operation? He was an outsider, at least to them."

"His company, Efficiency Consultants Incorporated, has a flawless reputation." She pushed the salad bowl toward him. "Have some more salad. At least the tomatoes are edible today." She chewed thoughtfully and swallowed before adding, "What puzzles me, though, is this vandalizing of equipment. That doesn't sound like E.C.I."

"There's no proof that he was behind the sabotage," Lukas pointed out. Running a crust of bread around his plate, he popped it into his mouth. "So, what's your idea on this murder?"

Anthea tilted her graying head, resting her chin in her palm. "Murder is a serious step to take, to get rid of an efficiency expert. Still, some of those fiercely independent Epirotis wouldn't have taken too kindly to an interloper coming into their village and telling them what to do. Tell me, Lukas, what's the sister like?"

He smiled. "What's she like? I don't quite know what I expected, given the family background, but I got a blond Amazon. Wiped out from the trip and not at her best under the influence of severe culture shock, but an Amazon nevertheless."

When a helpful flight attendant from her plane had pointed her out, he hadn't believed his eyes. At least five foot nine and slender, she had been dressed in narrow faded jeans and a fashionably loose silk shirt. High cheekbones gave distinction to a face a little too strong for true beauty, and the waves of tawny hair in a shade between brown and blond gave her the look of a lion. Well rested and on her own turf, she must be a stunner.

Only, he told himself now, she was not his type. He preferred small, cuddly brunettes.

"She impressed you," Anthea said, not missing his introspective silence.

"My, what all-seeing eyes you have, Mother." He gave her another slow grin. "She might impress me after a good night's sleep."

"Good," his mother said, taking a pear from a bowl of fruit on the table. "It's about time you met a woman who can do that."

He lifted one hand as if to fend her off. They had had this discussion before. "Don't start matchmaking, Mother. She's only here until she gets some information about her brother's death, and then she'll be gone." Pausing for maximum effect, he waited slyly until she looked up from the pear she was methodically slicing. "Don't bother with dinner for me. I told her I'd pick her up at seven."

"Ah," said Anthea, beginning to smile. "So you did like her."

"No way," he said too quickly, breaking off, flustered. "I mean, I guess she's nice enough. Just not my type."

"But dinner?"

He pushed back his chair, carrying his plate and the empty beer bottle to the sink. "We need to discuss the case." He dropped a brief kiss onto her cheek. "*Antío,* Mother. Have to get back to the office. Thanks for the lunch."

Anthea gazed after him thoughtfully as he loped out the door, stirring only when the squeal of tires told her he was gone.

IN SPITE OF HER INTENTION to at least go to the police station to check on the status of the investigation, Nadia slept away the afternoon. She woke with a start when the hotel room phone rang.

Pushing back her tangled hair with one hand, she groped for the phone with the other, bringing it with difficulty to her ear. "Yes?" Her voice was thick with sleep.

"Kýrios Stylianos is waiting in the lobby," the desk clerk informed her in his painfully correct English.

She held up her arm, squinting at her watch. Six fifty-five. Five to seven! All thought of sleep fled. Jerking to an upright position, she swiveled her eyes toward the window. The curtains were closed, but the quality of the twilight filtering through the loose weave confirmed the time.

"Kyría?" The desk clerk's voice sounded plaintive in her ears.

"Uh, tell him I'll be there in fifteen minutes."

"Very good, *Kyría.*"

Nadia pulled a face as she hung up. Greeks must be very astute judges of age. It hadn't escaped her that he'd used the Greek equivalent of madame. At home she was often still addressed as miss by taxi drivers and other strangers. At what age did a woman graduate from miss to madam? Thirty? Well, she'd passed that milestone a month ago.

Jumping out of bed, she selected fresh clothes from her open suitcase, taking them into the minuscule bathroom adjoining the room.

Stylianos, he of the quick smiles, amber eyes and hair-raising driving habits, was waiting. He didn't strike her as a particularly patient man. Well, fifteen minutes should be ample time to make herself presentable. It wasn't as if she had to impress him.

After a longing look at the shower, she settled for a quick face wash. She looked rested, her eyes once more clear, her skin restored to its normal color and tone. Her spirits also had recovered; she felt strong, confident. She *would* find Gerald's killer. She would make the uncomfortable alliance with Lukas Stylianos work to her advantage. While she had no desire to cause trouble for anyone but the guilty party, she was determined not to give up until she had the answer to every one of her questions.

Lukas sat on a bench at the side of the narrow, street-front lobby, thumbing through a brochure advertising a three-day bus tour that took in every major classical site on the Greek mainland. As Nadia stepped out of the creaking elevator, he jammed the brochure back into the rack on the wall and rose to meet her.

"That was quick." He glanced at his watch. "Fifteen minutes exactly. Am I right to assume you were still sleeping?" He tilted his head, staring into her face with disconcerting intensity. "It's done you a world of good."

Only a lingering fuzziness in her head reminded her that she had crossed ten time zones in the past twenty-four hours. "I feel better," she said, glad she'd taken the time to apply a little eye shadow and blusher. He was handsome, a fact she hadn't fully appreciated this morning. And he'd been assigned to help her. The idea that he was a watchdog, just waiting to pounce if she stepped on any official toes, now seemed an absurd fantasy brought on by fatigue. "Listen," she added, "I'm sorry for the way I behaved this morning. I was tired. And it was all so strange and intimidating."

"No problem," he said easily as he held the door for her. "Jet lag will do that. As long as you're feeling better now."

On the street, outside the relative quiet of the hotel lobby, the cacophony of the traffic could be heard. But the air was soft, the green scents of spring holding their own against the pervasive exhaust fumes. To Nadia it was exotic, exciting, a city pulsing with life, its ambience reeking more of the East than of the West.

"What kind of a car is this, anyway?" she asked as Lukas let her by the passenger door before walking around to the driver's side. "I know it's a Renault, but it's the strangest Renault I've ever seen, with those fenders that stick out and the engine growling behind us in the back seat."

Lukas twisted the key in the ignition. "It's an R5 Turbo. They only made a limited number of them. I was lucky to get one." He threw her a charming grin that lighted up his lean features. "Her name is Jolie." He glanced out of the side window, waiting until a taxi roared past, then pulled skillfully out of the cramped parking space he'd been lucky to get and into the stream of traffic. "Know much about cars?"

"Only that they have four wheels and an engine under the hood. Usually." She smiled, a gamine grin that momentarily stopped his breath. Maybe she was his type, after all. It wasn't as if he had to commit his life to her. "I've written copy for car brochures, but most of the stuff we used was centered on the options, the aesthetics, and the psychological buttons you push to make people want to buy."

"You're in advertising," he said, propelling the little car across an intersection under the frowning eyes of a helmeted motorcycle policeman. "Do you like it? I hear it's a high-pressure field."

"I wouldn't be doing it if I didn't like it," she informed him with a touch of acerbity. "And I like the pressure."

He grinned knowingly, with a expression that was so close to condescension that it infuriated her. "Oh, one of those. The high-powered career woman."

"Do you have a problem with that, Mr. Stylianos?" She bristled. Her remarkable mane of hair seemed to crackle with electricity.

With a quick twist of his wrist, he turned the car into a parking lot, sending up a billow of dust as the wheels spun in the dry sand. He braked sharply. "No, of course not. I don't have a problem with that. My mother's a lawyer. In our family, women have always had careers. But that doesn't mean they don't have time for their families and for pleasure."

The way the word pleasure rolled off his tongue put Nadia in mind of French vanilla ice cream on an August day. A peculiar tingle shivered through her stomach, and she fought down the blush she knew patched her cheeks.

Fortunately Lukas was occupied with receiving directions from the young parking attendant, an exchange that was incomprehensible to her. After what sounded like a argument, though smiles were stamped on their faces, they seemed to reach an agreement. Lukas set the car in motion at a sedate pace and parked next to the attendant's booth. He got out, locked his side of the car, then came around and helped Nadia out before locking her door. With a cocky grin at the young man, he tossed the keys into the air, expertly caught them, then took Nadia's arm and walked out of the lot with her.

"What was that all about?" Nadia asked, wishing that she either understood the language or at least was acquainted with the freewheeling nature of the people. It occurred to her for the first time to wonder how Gerald had managed. But of course he'd known the language. As for the culture, maybe blood counted for something. After all, his father had been Greek. And Gerald had been very attached to the country, considering it his home in spite of his Canadian upbringing.

"Nothing much. He wanted me to leave the key, as the sign there indicates." He gestured at the gate where a neat, black-lettered sign hung. "I told him I was a cop and might need the car in a hurry."

"Don't you trust him?" Nadia was torn between horror and fascination. A little research before her trip had informed her that Greece had very few criminals in jail, yet she'd seen traffic laws flouted at every opportunity.

He jingled the keys in his hand. "Well, yes and no. It's kind of like a game. If you can get away with it— We Greeks have never been known for our conformity."

Did murder come in the guise of nonconformity? Suddenly, despite the warmth of the evening and Lukas's hand under her elbow, a chill ran through her body.

As surely as if it had been written on the wall of the building in front of her, she knew that finding Gerald's killer was not going to be easy.

Chapter Two

The taverna where he took her was small, dim and smoky, in a cellar off a street in the Plaka so narrow that only two people could walk abreast. Both she and Lukas had to duck their heads under the lintel of the doorway at the bottom of the steps.

The music was loud, echoing off the low ceiling with the same cadence Nadia had heard on the tape in his car. A singer in a long flowing dress hugged a microphone to her lips and wailed mournfully in a minor key.

Not a single tourist sat at any of the tables, an observation Nadia did not find reassuring, especially as Lukas led her to a table in a dark corner farthest from the door.

Wondering what she was letting herself in for, Nadia took the chair he politely held for her. She glanced around the room as he seated himself on the side of the table adjacent to hers. Few of the other tables were occupied, and except for the singer and herself, the patrons were all male.

Lukas saw her eyes skew wildly, like those of a rabbit looking for escape from a trap. He smiled gently, covering her hand with one of his own, noting how cold her fingers were. Wrapping his own around them, he tried to convey reassurance. "Don't worry, Nadia. They're all my friends."

And indeed they must be, as several men waved across the smoke-hazed room and called out to him. Nadia forced a smile to her stiff lips, clinging to the heat of Lukas's hard fingers as she determined to look upon this as an adventure.

"Do you drink ouzo?" he asked her, still smiling, his eyes resting on her face.

Perhaps the fiery aperitif would settle her fluttering nerves. Nadia nodded. "I've had it."

"Would you like one now?"

She shrugged, realizing only then how rigidly she was holding her shoulders. "Why not?"

He squeezed her fingers as he lifted his other hand to summon the waiter. "Come on, Nadia, no one's going to bite you. Relax." He looked up as an old man with a sweeping gray mustache came up to the table. "Two ouzos, please, and two glasses of water."

The man nodded. "Right away, Kýrie Lukas."

Lukas turned back to her.

"So, Nadia," he said, "how much time have you allowed for what might well be a case that drags on for months?"

"I've taken an indefinite leave of absence." She gave him a hard stare. "What do you mean, it could drag on for months? Haven't you any leads at all?"

"We're following some now. But remember it's only been a week, and communication with the village where it happened is difficult, especially since the bridge on the only road there was washed out last week in a storm."

"You mean we can't get there?" Nadia exclaimed in consternation.

"I understand they've put up a temporary bridge. We'll be able to reach the village." He shifted in his chair, drumming his fingertips lightly on the table. "I would have gone already, but I was ordered to wait for you. I've been put in charge of this case, with the freedom to act as I see fit. And right now, I'm wondering about the wisdom of taking you to the scene of the crime."

She looked at him suspiciously, not wanting to hear a confirmation of her original fear that the authorities would try to obstruct her efforts to find Gerry's killer. "Are you refusing to let me go up there? I don't think you can stop me. There are always rental cars or buses." She broke off as the waiter returned.

"*Efharisto,* Panayioti." Lukas thanked the waiter before lifting his glass of ouzo. "Welcome to Greece, Nadia. I hope you'll find what you're looking for."

It was an odd toast in the light of their conversation. She lifted her own glass a little uncertainly, grimacing as the liquor burned its way down her throat.

"You're not used to it, are you?" he observed quietly. "Ouzo is a strong drink." He tipped one of the glasses of water over her ouzo, turning the clear liquid milky. "You'll like it better now."

What a strange man he was, she thought. One moment hard and tough, uncooperative, as if the last thing in the world he wanted was to baby-sit her. And then he would change, becoming kind and considerate, the perfect ambassador to introduce her to his native land and to insulate her from the inevitable difficulties she would encounter.

A party of about ten people, including a number of women, came down the stairs from the street, talking and laughing as they pulled tables together to form one large enough to accommodate them all. Lukas turned his head toward them, giving Nadia a chance to look at him unobserved.

He had changed from this morning's jeans and striped shirt to gray flannel trousers and a pale blue shirt with the sleeves rolled just to his elbows. The corded muscles of his forearms flexed under tanned skin that was liberally covered with silky black hair. He wore no tie, his shirt collar casually unbuttoned at the top. At the base of his throat hung a gold chain so fine it seemed spun from spiders' silk. It caught the light and flashed as he moved his head. The tiny cross that nestled in the hollow between his collarbones was nearly hidden in the black hair she realized must also cover his broad chest.

The tangled curls looked soft to the touch.

Hurriedly Nadia banished the wholly inappropriate thought. She had been brought up in a family who weren't touchers. During her childhood she had experienced little physical contact, no public displays of affection. She couldn't remember ever seeing her mother kiss her father. It just wasn't done.

The emotionally sterile appearance of the marriage made it difficult for Nadia to accept her dormant sensuality. She'd tapped it for the first time during her year-long relationship with Dorian, the one man in her life she'd been serious about. Dorian had been a toucher, one of a family of Greek-Canadians who believed in closeness, a quality she had embraced with all the curbed passion in her. Perhaps that was why she'd closed her eyes to the signs that should have warned her their relationship couldn't last.

The family unity she had so enjoyed had ultimately been shattered. Although the hurt had faded, it was a lesson she would be wise to keep in mind in her dealings with Lukas.

She brought her eyes up to his face. In the strong planes of his cheeks and jaw she saw character, control and an alertness that she sensed could erupt into action, should that be necessary. Still, there was a sensitivity about his mouth that was at odds with the latent toughness.

And then there were those remarkable eyes glowing in the dim light, a molten gold that mesmerized her.

He was watching her, a half smile on his lips. She realized he'd probably noticed her staring at him. To cover her embarrassment she said the first thing that came into her head. "Where did you learn your English?"

His smile remained, warm, understanding, as if he knew the confusion of her thoughts. "Mostly in England. We used to go there a lot when my father was alive. And I spent a couple of summers with relatives in Boston and in Montreal."

"So you've been all over?" she asked.

"A few places," he agreed. "I still travel sometimes. One of my sisters lives in London, England, the other in Toronto. So I'm familiar with Canada."

Listening to his low voice, Nadia realized that he was far from being the standard city cop who knew nothing outside his own cultural experience. He had

had a cosmopolitan upbringing that must serve him well in his dealings with the tourists. No wonder he was considered special. She was suddenly ashamed of her earlier resentment of him. She should be grateful they'd assigned him to her case. He could help her.

As if he had read her thoughts, he said quietly, "We're on the same side, Nadia. Remember that."

That was precisely what she'd found hard to accept. "Are we?"

"Of course we are." The words were spoken with conviction.

Most of the tables around them were occupied now as the late Athens dinner hour approached. Although the clientele was still predominantly male, Nadia no longer felt herself the focus of all eyes. After a brief intermission the vocalist was back singing her melancholy ballads, which Nadia was beginning to enjoy. Between numbers the singer chatted with customers, obviously acquaintances, who sat near the small stage. The atmosphere was lively, yet comfortable.

Out of the corner of his eye, Lukas saw a lone man come down the stairs. He ducked under the doorway, even though his stature hardly warranted the precaution. Short and stocky, with a head of grizzled curls and ample jowls in need of a shave, he looked like the sort of working-class man whom tavernas such as this had originally served. Lukas's eyes narrowed as he followed the man's progress to an unoccupied table at the far side of the room. He looked familiar. There was a somewhat arrogant tilt of his head that was at odds with the shiny, unfashionable suit he wore. He walked with a faint limp. Where had Lukas seen him?

He dismissed the question as Panayioti came to take their dinner order.

Nadia watched as Lukas took charge. Familiar with Greek food, thanks to Dorian, she was sure anything Lukas ordered would please her.

"Were you close to your brother, Nadia?" Lukas asked when they were alone again. "The age difference couldn't have been much."

"He was my half brother. Six years older. I'm thirty."

His brows rose slightly. She didn't look it, and yet she did. A youthful face paired with an aura of competence and maturity, giving her a womanliness that, despite his words to his mother, appealed to him. She was slender, but curved in the right places, although he could only guess at the exact contours of her breasts, disguised as they were by the loose-fitting yellow shirt she wore now.

She displayed an almost fierce independence, a determination that worried him a little. Her brother had been murdered. Whoever was guilty might not take kindly to her poking around. They'd killed once—the second time was always easier.

He suppressed a rising frustration. He couldn't stop her, wasn't even sure he wanted to, since he could empathize with her need to know what had happened.

He had to protect her. But what made him uncomfortable were feelings that transcended professional detachment.

He found himself drawn to her with something more than sympathy. Was it the exuberance of her tawny hair, now brushed back from her face but still as unruly as a lion's mane? Or the slumberous quality that sometimes came into her eyes, their clarity made exotic by the ring of black that surrounded the dark blue iris? Perhaps it was the faint scent of a musky perfume that held a hint of Oriental mystery. The aroma, evident even in the smoky air of the crowded room, teased him every time she moved. He kept feeling an urge to get closer to her, to discover its source, to find the shape of her body under the concealing folds of her shirt.

She spoke, jarring him out of his increasingly erotic reverie.

"As for whether we were close, during our childhood, we were probably closer than most siblings since there were just the two of us, and our parents were very busy. In the last few years, although we corresponded, we saw less of each other. Still, that's to be expected when people grow up. We each had our own lives." *Lives. Unfortunate thought.* Gerald no longer had his.

Her eyes clouded over and she shuddered as she thought of the violence that had stalked Gerald. "You've no idea what a shock it was to learn that he was dead. And not only dead, but murdered in a brutal fashion. Lukas, his killer must be found."

The sound of his name spoken by her low, faintly husky voice ran warmly through him. Inappropriately, he thought, but he did nothing to cool the feeling. *Yes,* despite the uneasiness that had marked their association so far, he decided he liked her. Although he sensed she felt at a disadvantage in the strange environment, after her initial nervousness she had apparently overcome her feeling of intimidation. Briefly he regretted his impulse to bring her here rather than take her to the more mundane surroundings of, say, a French restaurant in Kolonaki. He admitted his motives hadn't been the best; he'd been testing her.

And what had he found? That she was adaptable. And courageous, more so than any woman he knew. Without knowing the language, she had come to a strange country to find out why her brother had died. She had courage and loyalty in equal portions.

"Tell me, what was your brother like?"

The question startled her. "You mean you don't know?"

"Well, since the first time I heard of him he was already dead, I couldn't know, could I?"

"No, I guess not." She toyed for a moment with her fork as she gathered her thoughts. What could she tell him? She thought she knew Gerry as well as anyone had, but in reality he'd seldom discussed his work, in which he had seemed highly successful and which had frequently involved travel.

She wished now she knew more about this last trip. Surely calculating a more cost-efficient way to quarry marble wouldn't lead to murder.

Not that it would have done much good to question him. For all his easygoing exterior, Gerald had possessed a stubborn streak she'd never been able to defeat. If he didn't want to discuss something, he clammed up.

The clatter of cutlery brought her mind back to the present. Their food had arrived. Determinedly pushing aside her futile self-reproach, she picked up her fork once more and took a bite of the spicy moussaka, chewing thoughtfully. "It's very good."

Lukas smiled. "Yes, it is. I knew you'd like it." He ate in silence for a moment, then said, "Tell me about your brother."

"Efficiency Consultants Incorporated did well, according to his letters. But he never talked much about his work. There was something secretive about him whenever I brought up the subject." Put this way, her words suddenly struck her as smacking of disloyalty. Gerry was dead. But perhaps his very reticence might prove to be the most serious obstacle she would have to overcome. To give herself a moment, she gulped from the wineglass before her, welcoming the astringent bite of the retsina.

"Secretive?" Lukas asked. "In what way?"

"The company was based here in Athens, but he traveled all over the world," she said. "He never talked much about what they did."

Lukas's brows rose. "I thought you were close."

She frowned. "We were, but when we saw each other we didn't discuss work." She set down her wineglass with a thump. "But no matter what he did, he didn't deserve to die."

He inclined his head. "No, he didn't. At least we agree on that." The singer's voice, rough and evocative of lonely nights and too many cigarettes, filled the silence between them.

Nadia broke it. "Are we going straight up to the village where—" She closed her eyes for an instant, tears burning. "The village where it happened? Will we go there tomorrow?"

Lukas stared thoughtfully into the middle distance. "Nadia, did Gerald ever mention an island called Atalanti?"

She creased her brow. "You don't mean Atlantis, do you? I thought that was a myth."

"That may be, but this is a real place, a speck in the Ionian Sea between the mainland and Kérkira. Oh, sorry, you call it Corfu. It's almost within sight of the Albanian coast."

Nadia shook her head. "I've never heard of it. Has this got something to do with Gerald's death?"

Lukas wrapped his fingers around the stem of his wineglass. "That's what we'd like to know. We know your brother went there about a week before his death. He stayed a couple of days, then returned to Pefkaki, the village where he was killed. We haven't been able to find out whom he saw on the island." He twirled the glass, his eyes on the wine that seemed to catch and hold the light from the candle on the table. "The island is dying, like so many of its sort, isolated from adjoining land and with little industry. And what happened there in 1948 was tragic." He lifted his eyes to meet Nadia's. "Your brother wouldn't have used his consulting firm to cover up something else, would he?"

A chill seeped into her stomach. She was uncertain whether it was fear or anger. What was Lukas suggesting? That her brother was deceptive, a liar? Remembering the Greek policeman was there to help, Nadia shook her head.

"I don't know, Lukas." Her hair swung on her shoulders. "I just don't know."

She pushed away her plate, her appetite gone. "Lukas, what have you found out so far? I think I have a right to know."

Shifting restlessly in his chair, he set his plate aside, as well. "If you want the truth, we have exactly nothing. His body was found near the quarry, the morning after he was killed. He had a meeting with his men, but after that was over, no one knows what possessed him to leave the village late at night. He was in the building where he rented a room until nearly midnight, then he went out alone, according to witnesses. But there is always the possibility of a cover-up. Those Epirotis are a closemouthed, independent lot. They don't air their dirty linen before outsiders."

Nadia felt despair dragging down the hope she'd briefly entertained. Sally, her mother, had lived in Greece in her youth and had mentioned the ferociously insular life-style of the remote villages. "So there's not much hope of a break in the case. It really could go on for months or even years."

Lukas shrugged, in a manner that struck her as particularly fatalistic. "That's what I said. But there's always hope. Once we get to Pefkaki, we'll be better able to assess what we're up against." Straightening in his chair, he drained his glass and signaled for the check. "Any idea what possessed him to go to the village in the first place? Yeah, I know. The quarry. But how did he come to hear of it? It wouldn't have been a story covered by *Time*."

"I have no idea. The last letter I had from him said he was working in the village. No hint of anything but a simple job that might last several months. A day later, the consulate informed me he'd been killed." Grief caught at Nadia's throat and she rubbed her hand over her eyes. "There was no reason to suspect he might be in danger. But I can't help feeling there should have been something. If only I knew more about his business, or his personal life—"

Lukas covered her hand with his, holding it for a moment before she pulled away. "Don't waste time feeling guilty. None of us can control another's destiny, and it's presumptuous to think otherwise. It's all in God's hands."

Her eyes widened in surprise as she looked at him. "That's odd. That's what Gerry always used to say, too. He had a peculiar philosophy of predestination that didn't go with his upbringing."

Lukas grinned, the bright flash of his teeth dispelling solemnity. "I'm like him?"

Although she knew the question was whimsical, she considered it seriously. In some ways he was. Like Gerry, Lukas had integrity, a quality she saw too little of in the world of advertising, where illusion masqueraded as reality. And in other ways? Well, Lukas certainly didn't have the charming innocence that had often characterized Gerry. "No, I think you're a much more complex man." Lifting her blue eyes, she fixed him with a candid stare. "And I think I'm going to like working with you."

It was obvious that he hadn't expected this degree of honesty from her. Surprise flashed in his eyes, then they grew serious. "Don't get too confident. I have a weird feeling about this whole thing, and we may never find the answers."

"As long as we find the killer," Nadia said grimly.

He shrugged and paid the check. "We'll see."

On the way to the door, Lukas steered a path through the room that took them past the table where the man in the shiny suit was peeling an apple with a sharp little knife. As they drew near, the man paused in his task and lifted his head. His eyes were a peculiarly opaque green, like malachite pebbles, and the malevolence in them sent a chill up Lukas's spine.

Where *had* he seen the man before?

He nodded curtly, and the man looked down. The knife sliced into the crisp apple, severing a chunk that was half core. Lukas received the distinct impression that the almost vicious gesture had been for his benefit, a warning.

Committing the man's appearance to memory, taking particular note of the faint outline of a scar near his temple, Lukas continued toward the door. A sidelong glance at Nadia told him she'd noticed nothing out of the ordinary.

And perhaps there hadn't been. He stepped outside and inhaled the distinctive scent of an Athens night, the composite of diesel fumes, roasted coffee and dust. He wondered if the incident had been only a product of his far too active imagination.

"Would you like to see Gerald's apartment?" he asked. "It's not far."

Nadia lifted her head, her eyes losing their melancholy. "Could we? Maybe we'll find something there."

Lukas shook his head. "I doubt it. The police have already been over it, and I looked at it myself after I came into the case."

They walked in silence four blocks to an undistinguished building bordering the Plaka. The tiny rooms on the ground floor seemed claustrophobic, the close heat trapped inside them making it difficult to breathe. Nadia opened a window, realizing as soon as she did so that it was a mistake. The roar of traffic on its relentless surge up to the Acropolis rolled into the room with a deafening cacophony.

Lukas was right. The flat, consisting of a living room, kitchen and bedroom, with a minuscule bath tucked away at the back, had the impersonal look of a hotel suite. Rummaging through the desk yielded only paid electrical bills and receipts for the apartment rent, both in incomprehensible Greek, nothing of significance. Nadia found her letters to Gerald, neatly put away in an old shoe box, along with snapshots of their parents and herself. On the night table in the bedroom stood a framed photo of all four of them, taken at Nadia's university graduation.

She stared at it. Had she really been that young, that optimistic?

"You've changed," Lukas commented at her back, his presence conveying warmth and understanding, yet not quite comfort. The awareness of their task and its difficulty loomed between them, precluding real intimacy.

"Yes," she agreed, putting down the picture and wrapping her arms around her chest.

"Did Gerald change too, since then?"

Nadia glanced back at the smiling face, the keen eyes and well-defined features. A square chin and a prominent nose gave his face a cast that inspired confidence. This man knew where he was going and how to get there. "No, he didn't change much, except perhaps that he looked a bit older."

She went back into the living room, braving the traffic noise that poured in through the open window. The moon had risen and the ravaged columns of the Parthenon glowed with a gentle luminance in its light.

"Maybe the view makes up for the noise," she muttered.

"You get used to it," Lukas said, pulling out the bottom drawers of the desk. They were empty. That still puzzled him. But then the man seemed to have left his business at the office.

"Gerry loved Greece," Nadia said pensively, her voice carrying an undertone of sadness. "I think he spent more time here as an adult than he did in Canada, or in any of the other countries his work took him to."

"Is that why he was buried in Epirus?" Lukas asked, coming up beside her. "I wondered about that."

Nadia frowned. "He often talked about the mountains, the awesome yet beautiful desolation. The country seemed to have a fascination for him." Her voice dropped until Lukas could barely hear her. "I wonder if he knew he would die young. Most people his age don't give a thought to where they'd like to be buried."

"Maybe he did. It all points to a secret life that no one knew about." He held her hand in his, releasing it when she pulled away. "We'll find the truth."

They were silent as they left the apartment and crossed the road. The Plaka streets lay like random paths around them, filled with dark, mysterious shadows since, due to the banning of neon lights, the only illumination came from widely spaced street lamps.

Few people were about. Although Athens was noted for the liveliness of its night life, Holy Week and the reality of a workday tomorrow had emptied the tavernas soon after midnight.

A black cat stalked across the cobbled lane, pausing in a doorway to gaze inscrutably at them, its eyes a lambent green in the moonlight.

"Witch's cat," Nadia muttered.

Lukas looked at her with a quizzical half smile. "Superstitions? I'm surprised at you."

"I don't believe in them," she protested mildly. "But he looks like the cats in the Halloween stories we read as kids."

The cat yawned, displaying needle-pointed fangs and a rosy tongue. It sat back on its haunches and began to wash its face with a lifted paw.

Lukas and Nadia resumed their leisurely pace. When she stumbled slightly, he took her hand. To his surprise, she allowed the contact.

They had almost passed the cat when it pricked up its ears and let out a yowl, then streaked off down the street, fanning out its tail like a bottle brush. Before they had quite recovered from the startling shriek, a blinding light stopped them in their tracks. With an angry snarl a car was upon them, and Lukas had only time to jerk Nadia out of the way before it roared past.

Nursing a bruised arm, Nadia sagged against the rough stucco wall of a building. Her heart pounded in her throat; her knees felt like overcooked spaghetti. For once she had no urge to pull away from Lukas's hold. The warm solidity of his body represented safety, protection.

It was a moment before she realized that he was speaking in a low, vicious tone, swearing, she assumed, at jerks who sped late at night down a twisting, narrow street.

"I knew it," he said finally. "I knew I'd seen him before."

"What are you talking about?" Nadia stood trapped between his chest and the wall behind her, held protectively by his arms. The scent of soap and an elusive after-shave teased her, making her aware of him as she had not been of a man for a very long time. She went to move away but his arms tightened.

"Damn it, I won't hurt you. Stand still. Are you hurt?"

"Just my arm. But I think it's only bruised."

He rolled up her sleeve, muttering at the tear in the sweater she'd put on over her shirt. His fingers were warm and gentle as he probed the tender spot on her arm. "Skin's not broken, as far as I can tell." Tentatively he bent her elbow and then her wrist. "Hurt at all?"

She shook her head, then realized he probably couldn't see the movement in the darkness. "No, it's okay."

Almost against his will, he inhaled the fragrance of her hair as it brushed across his face, the faint sweet muskiness that seemed the essence of femininity. He wanted to bury his face in it, feel her skin beneath his mouth.

He pulled back, shaken by the strength of the urge and the unexpected tenderness he felt. He had been prepared to take her up to Epirus, more or less go through the motions of satisfying her that he was doing everything he could to find her brother's killer, but now it was more real, more personal. He had seen her grief, felt the love she'd had for Gerald. He would do his best to help her.

Nadia was staring at him, her expression bewildered, and he wondered what she saw in his face. She trembled slightly, as if a cool wind had chased over her skin.

"We'll have to be more careful." His voice was hoarse, and he cleared his throat.

"Yes." She shivered again, thinking of the malevolent harshness of the light that had impaled them. An accident? Obviously Lukas didn't think so.

"Tell me," she said as they moved away from the building, "what did you mean, you'd seen him before?"

Too long used to keeping his own counsel, he briefly considered prevaricating. But there didn't seem to be much point, especially since she would find out soon enough that they might well be in danger.

Correction. *She* might be in danger.

"That car followed us from the airport this morning. In all that traffic I barely noticed. But when I saw the man eating by himself in the restaurant tonight, I wondered if I'd seen him before. I'd seen him all right, in the rearview mirror when we were crawling along Syngrou. The car tonight was the one I saw him driving this morning." He hurried Nadia off the deserted street and into the parking lot. "I think he deliberately tried to run us down."

Chapter Three

Nadia's mind was reeling and she could only stare at him. "You mean," she gasped, "that wasn't just some idiot driving too fast on a city street?"

"No. And it won't seem so surprising to you, when you realize this street is closed to automobile traffic."

Nadia's agile brain added this latest revelation to the other facts she had. "That means that there might be more to this than simply a murder in a remote village."

"Murder is never simple, especially an apparently cold-blooded murder." Lukas bent to unlock the car. "Most murders here are crimes of passion, done in the heat of anger."

Nadia got in on the passenger side, pulling her seat belt across and snapping it securely. "Do you suppose the motive behind Gerald's death could have been something like that?"

Lukas shook his head as he inserted the key into the ignition. "No, this appears to be different." The engine roared into life, settling to a throbbing purr. "The villagers may have resented Gerald's presence, but there are no indications that he had any one particular enemy."

"But it could have been, especially if a woman were involved," Nadia said, more for the sake of argument than anything else. They had to consider all possibilities, no matter how remote.

Lukas shrugged dismissively. "Gerry had hardly been there long enough to begin a relationship. And there was no gossip." The tires squeaked as he accelerated onto the street. "In villages gossip is more reliable than a newspaper. Did he date much? My impression is that he kept to himself. We didn't find an address book. There were no indications of a life outside his work."

"He was a very private man," Nadia said, trying to remember specific women Gerald might have mentioned in his letters to her. She couldn't recall a single name. Of course that didn't mean much. "But yes, he dated."

"Strange he wasn't married, even though he was thirty-six. Were any of his relationships serious?"

Were they? She couldn't remember. But even when he was in Vancouver, he'd seldom brought his friends to meet her. "I'm not sure," she admitted. "He knew a lot of people but rarely brought them home. He was the type to go out to meet his friends and girlfriends in town. I was his little sister, so I didn't tag along."

Lukas looked serious. "Maybe it is something worth investigating. He might have met a woman, angered a brother or father who covered it up so that she wouldn't be gossiped about. They're pretty protective of their women up there."

She didn't want to admit the same thought had occurred to her. "That's just it. We don't know. But I have to say it's possible." She broke off, frowning. "That doesn't explain why someone is following us."

Lukas scowled at the windshield as he braked in front of Nadia's hotel. "No, it doesn't, and I'd certainly like to know what the hell is going on."

Stepping out onto the street, he locked the door and walked around to her side, putting out his hand to help her from the car. "Nadia, have you unpacked your things?"

She paused, peripherally aware of the warmth and strength of his fingers around hers. "No, I haven't. This morning I was too tired and this evening in too much of a hurry."

He grinned faintly at the unconscious admission. She could have kept him waiting; she'd been under no obligation to cooperate. She could have refused to see him. The fact that she'd hurried told him she had wanted to have dinner with him. Then she threw cold water on that notion by adding, "I was afraid you'd leave without giving me the information you had about Gerry. And what difference does it make whether I unpacked?"

"Because it'll save time when you check out."

She gaped at him. "Why should I check out? Just because a car nearly hit us on the street doesn't mean I'm in any danger here. I'll lock my door."

"You're part of my assignment," he said with what he hoped was a professional detachment. "I'd feel much better if I had you where I can keep an eye on you until we leave for Pefkaki. At my house. And before you get on your high horse and go all virtuous on me, you'll be happy to know we'll be well chaperoned. By my mother."

"You live with your mother?"

He shrugged. "Sure. What's wrong with that? She's alone and the house is big enough. Besides, I happen to like my mother. Does that make me a wimp?"

She looked him up and down, noting his height, the lean muscularity of his frame, remembering how solid he'd felt pressed against her when he'd pushed her out of the path of the speeding car. "No," she said softly. "You're not a wimp."

He slammed the car door, giving her an odd look. "Well, I'm relieved. You noticed."

KNOWING HIS MOTHER PLANNED to go to her office that day, Lukas made a point of rising early the next morning. He found her sitting at the kitchen table, eating the gruesome concoction of granola and stewed fruit that was her breakfast.

"Mother, I've brought Nadia here to stay until we leave for Pefkaki."

Her jaw dropped, and the spoon fell with a clatter into the almost empty bowl. "You've what?"

He slammed one cupboard door and opened another in a futile search for a cup for his coffee. "You heard me. Nadia's here. Where the hell have you put the cups?"

"In the next cupboard. I cleaned yesterday afternoon."

"You could have put things back where they belong," he grumbled, without knowing why he bothered. She got these urges to rearrange her surroundings about three times a year. He should be used to it by now.

"I thought it would be more efficient that way."

"More confusing, you mean," he muttered, setting the cup on the counter. After a search through more cupboards, he found a pot, added water and an egg, and set it on the stove to boil. "On second thought, maybe I should cook two." He dropped in another, adjusting the gas under the pot.

"And where is Nadia now?" his mother asked with a pointed stare at the door through which he'd entered the kitchen. "In your room?"

"Mother! I've only just met the woman." He gave her a disgusted look as he leaned back, resting his hips against the edge of the counter.

"Sounds like you're making fast progress," Anthea said dryly. "Yesterday you didn't even like her."

"Yesterday I didn't know her." He turned around to pour out strong black coffee from the coffeepot on the stove, adding a spoonful of sugar, then another for good measure. "She's in the spare bedroom."

Anthea spooned the last of the granola into her mouth. "I hope you put fresh sheets on the bed."

"Of course I did," he said impatiently. "I gave her first use of the bathroom, and while she was in there I fixed the bed. You were asleep." His tone bordered on accusation.

"After midnight?" Anthea lifted delicate black brows. "I should hope so. I'm getting too old to stay up until all hours and work the next day."

"So I guess you'll miss the chance to meet her. You're going to work and we're leaving today."

Anthea looked at her watch. "I can wait until she gets up. I'd like to meet the first woman my son has brought home in years."

"Mother," he warned. "It's not like that." The water boiled and he let it simmer for a moment before removing the pot and running cold water over the eggs. Taking bread out of the bread box, he sat down at the table.

"It's always like that."

He conceded her point with a sheepish grin. "Okay, I admit it. The lady has a lot of guts. I like her. If I didn't, I would have just put her into a different hotel." He became serious. "I think someone doesn't want her brother's death investigated. I think they're trying to scare her off."

Between bits of his breakfast, he briefly related the events of the evening and gave her his analysis of them. When he finished, Anthea nodded. "Although it might have appeared simple on the surface, I didn't think a murder would ever be that straightforward. There's something behind this."

"That's what I think too. I have this weird feeling—"

Anthea's eyes narrowed as she gave him a shrewd look. "Maybe it's unrequited lust."

Lukas laughed in exasperation. "What kind of a mother are you, to accuse your only son of such a thing?"

"As you young people seem to forget so easily, we senior citizens were young once, too. We don't forget that easily."

"Well, as long as this investigation goes on, I'll keep a lid on whatever it is. If there really is a danger to her, I'd better keep on my toes. I can't let her distract me."

"It won't be easy." Anthea got up to take her bowl to the sink. "Especially if it's meant to be."

Now what did she mean by that? He didn't get a chance to ask her, as Nadia came into the room.

This morning, despite her height and the self-assured set of her shoulders, she looked young and vulnerable. Her hair curled in tawny disarray around her face, as if she'd brushed it but made no attempt at styling. She wore no makeup, the rosiness of naked skin giving her an innocence he sensed was not a facade. A faint pink crease on her cheek told Lukas she had slept soundly, and that she possessed little if any vanity.

She wore a tank top and running shorts, revealing long slender legs that were faintly tanned, possibly the remnants of last summer's sun, since he didn't think a person could do much tanning in Vancouver's notoriously wet winters. Her skin had a smooth creaminess he ached to touch.

The body-shaping clothes answered one of his questions of last night. She had a figure. *Oh, very definitely.* Her breasts were small but firm and perfectly shaped, her waist and hips slender yet pleasingly feminine. The memory of every voluptuous brunette Lukas had known was forever erased from his mind by the sight of Nadia's healthy blond radiance.

What kind of an ass he would have made of himself he was fortunately never to find out, as Anthea saw Nadia standing in the doorway.

"Good morning. You must be Nadia," she said in English as fluent as Lukas's. She smiled readily, but Nadia couldn't help noting the keen appraisal in the older woman's bright eyes as she looked at her. Apparently, though, she passed inspection, for Lukas's mother added, "Welcome to our house."

"Thank you, Mrs. Stylianos," Nadia replied. "I hope I haven't inconvenienced you, but Lukas insisted."

Anthea waved her hand. "Please call me Anthea. Lukas was right to insist."

"Thank you." Waking in the strange room early that morning, Nadia had lain in bed for a long time, worrying about her reception by Lukas's mother. In Canada people just didn't invite virtual strangers into their houses. She worried that Lukas would regret his gesture and that his mother would be displeased at having an uninvited guest foisted on her.

Nadia was relieved to see that she was truly welcome. Anthea was apparently a direct woman who knew her own mind and rarely wasted time questioning decisions.

Nadia turned now to the man sitting quietly at the table. "Good morning, Lukas. I'd like to go out for a run, and was wondering if there's time before the Canadian Embassy opens. I've got to check in with them before we head north."

She'd been aware of his scrutiny a moment ago, refusing to let it ruffle her composure. But she couldn't control the warmth that ran through her as he smiled the slow smile he used to such devastating effect, and allowed his gaze to move in leisurely fashion up her legs, linger at her breasts and then travel higher until he met her eyes.

"It opens at eight." He glanced at his watch. "It's barely seven now, so you've plenty of time." Abandoning his plate and the half-eaten egg on it, he pushed himself to his feet. "If you'll wait a moment for me to change, I'll join you."

Anthea cleared her throat. "Well, I must be off, children. You're leaving today, Lukas? Drive carefully, then." She glanced at Nadia. "Don't give Nadia a heart attack from Jolie's antics. Nadia, I hope I'll see you when you return. And I wish both of you success."

She paused as she passed Lukas, reaching up to plant a light kiss on his cheek. "Take care, *agapi mou*."

Turning her head, she smiled at Nadia. "You too, Nadia."

THEY WALKED at a brisk pace to a nearby high school, where Lukas suggested the cinder track would make a better running surface than the often uneven concrete and marble-block sidewalks. The playing field, green with new spring grass, was deserted.

"What time does school start?" Nadia asked curiously.

Lukas grinned, his teeth flashing sexily in his dark lean face. "Not this early. Anyway, they have the week off, for Easter. Don't you have spring break in Canada?"

"Oh, of course."

They started off around the track. Lukas, in spite of his admission that he didn't run as often as he should, easily matched Nadia's limber strides.

"You don't look out of shape to me," she panted as he increased their speed on their fifth circuit of the track. He was barely breathing deeply, and he looked cool, as if he could keep it up all day. Sweat poured down her body, soaking her top as the sun rose higher in the sky and beat down upon their heads.

"Don't forget you're probably still a bit jet-lagged. And you're not used to the climate." He grinned again, challenging her. "Want to quit?"

She put on a burst of speed, overtaking him. "No, I never quit."

"No, I don't suppose you do," she heard him mutter as he came pounding along behind her.

But in the end he passed her, bounding around the last bend of the track, his corded thigh and calf muscles covered with deeply tanned skin and fine black hair. Nadia faltered in her stride, recovering instantly, her face burning with a heat that owed little to exertion. He was a policeman, appointed to help her find her brother's killer, for Pete's sake, and here she was gazing at him like an impressionable adolescent.

"Slowpoke." He tossed the childish epithet over his shoulder.

Pushing herself to the limit, her shoes making rhythmic smacking sounds on the track surface, she managed to decrease his lead slightly. And when he slowed to glance back at her, she found a reserve of strength to shoot past him, panting in triumph. "Beat you."

"This once," he said, his smile complacent, his long lashes fluttering over clear amber eyes as he winked at her.

NEITHER OF THEM noticed the car parked around the corner, or the man whose flat green eyes followed them as they headed back toward the house. As soon as they were out of sight, the man left his car and entered a coffee shop just opening for the morning's business. Nodding at the owner, he went to the pay phone, dropping in a handful of coins. "This Stylianos doesn't look as if he'll be a threat," he said without preamble when the connection went through.

"Don't underestimate him," the voice at the other end warned. "He's their best investigator. They use him for all international incidents. He located that group of terrorists who were hiding out in Lávrion last year."

The green-eyed man couldn't contain his surprise. "It was never in the papers."

"Exactly. That shows his power. He's the best. His presence on the case indicates that someone knew Parker was onto something big. If we want to get out of this, we'd better take serious steps to cover our asses."

The man in the coffee shop laughed nastily. "Yeah, we'd better. So what do you want me to do, get rid of them permanently?" Pushing a hand into one pocket, he fingered the knife he carried, caressing the smooth ivory handle with a lover's touch, picturing the gleam of the naked blade in the instant before it slid with silky precision into human flesh.

There was a moment of silence, broken only by the buzzing of the phone lines. "Not yet. It would be too obvious. I don't want any more inconvenient cops nosing around, at least not for a few days. By then they won't find anything. However, an accident might not be remiss. We can't afford any more slipups."

AS IF the shared exercise had broken down some barrier between them, Nadia found herself far too aware of Lukas's nearness as they walked back to cool down. Whenever their eyes met or their hands accidentally touched, she felt a tingle of attraction that was disconcerting, to say the least. Under any other circumstances it might have been exhilarating. As it was, any interference with her stated purpose would only delay the investigation. Didn't Lukas realize that, or didn't he care?

But by the time they were inside, he seemed to have regained his professionalism. "You can use the bathroom first," he told her with the cool courtesy of a good host. "And there's still a boiled egg in the kitchen if you want something to eat."

"Thanks." Her tone was only faintly ironic.

"Don't spend an hour primping," he added. "I suppose you'd like to check at the police station as well, before we leave town, although it's not really necessary."

Nadia nodded. "Yes, I would." She gave him a steady, no-nonsense look. "I was told to check with them, and the Canadian Embassy. I'm not doing this on a whim. Will it take a lot of time?"

His annoyance appeared to clear. "Shouldn't."

"I'd also like to stop by Gerry's office," she added crisply. "I presume it's still in operation?"

"Yeah, there's someone there. But everything they could tell us is in the police report you must have seen."

"Even so, I'd like to see for myself."

"Okay." He sounded faintly impatient. "But after that, I'd like to get started. We can get some lunch later, on the road."

"That's fine with me," Nadia said. "Lukas, please understand. I'm just as anxious to get going as you, but I was told there were certain procedures."

"Bureaucrats," he muttered as he went down the hall.

It was already after eight, Nadia realized, glancing at her watch. After a stop in her room for fresh clothes, she turned on the shower in the bathroom, stripped and stepped under it. The hot water, coming from the nozzle with a much gentler rush than she was used to, flowed over her skin, subtly stimulating dormant nerve endings.

Face it, she told herself bluntly. *You like the guy.* But it would be the worst kind of folly to give in to the feeling.

Angrily she slammed the hot tap shut and twisted the other to full blast, shuddering as an icy deluge pelted her. *Stupid,* that was what she was, letting the first man who showed an attraction to her make her lose her senses. Shivering violently, she stepped from the shower and wrapped a thick towel around her goose-fleshed body. Gerald was dead, colder than she was at the moment. She was here to find his killer. Nothing could be allowed to distract her from that object, not even an attractive Greek with mesmerizing cat's eyes.

The house seemed empty and silent as she stepped into the hall. Where was Lukas? She had expected him to be waiting impatiently outside the door of the only bathroom in the house, but the narrow corridor was deserted.

Suddenly she heard a sound and a chill crept eerily up her spine. The sound faded away, and she shook her head, her hair swinging around her shoulders. Was the house haunted? She could have sworn she'd heard a ghostly flute playing Bach's "Air on a G String." Her mother's insistence on piano lessons had given her a formidable and, she often thought, largely irrelevant repertoire of classical music.

Moving under a compulsion she didn't even question, she walked silently down the hall just as the music resumed. This time it was an unfamiliar tune that sounded as ephemeral as the wind playing across a summer meadow.

Stealthily she pushed at a door that stood ajar at the end of the hall, bracing herself for the sight of an empty room.

The fanciful notion that the music was played by an invisible ghost was immediately dispelled by the sight of Lukas sitting cross-legged on the floor of a cluttered studio in a pool of brilliant sunshine.

The haunting song came from a silver flute that he held to his lips and played with such absorbed concentration he hadn't yet become aware of her presence.

For a moment Nadia stood in the doorway, frozen by her own bewilderment. At the age of thirty-one he lived in his mother's house, he played an instrument many considered too effeminate for a man, and he worked in a profession where only the strong, the toughest, survived.

Obviously he was a man whose complexities she hadn't begun to plumb. She should have had a premonition earlier, when he had looked at her and smiled with that sensuous mouth that could be both tender and willful at the same time. But caught in an ill-advised enchantment, she had just accepted the moment.

She would have to be on her guard at all times—

He finished with a last softly breathed note that hung on a slanting sunbeam long after he put down the flute. "Finished your shower?" he asked. "Good. Then I'll go." She watched his deft movements as he dismantled the flute, cleaned it, and placed it in a case lined with blue velvet. Those lean fingers, gentle yet strong, mesmerized her. *Crazy,* she thought, tearing her eyes away.

She looked about the cavernous room, moving around him to the easel that stood near the windows. "Do you paint, too?"

He smiled at her over his shoulder. "Not me. That's my mother's hobby. What do you think of it?"

Nadia was torn between honesty and tact. "I don't know much about art—" A subtle bending of the truth.

Lukas sprang to his feet. "Go ahead and say it. She hasn't any talent, has she? But she likes painting, says it relaxes her, and she never tries to make us hang any of her art."

"That's very considerate of her." Nadia fought to suppress a smile at the sight of a landscape that looked like an imprint from a used paint rag. Not for the world would she have risked hurting Anthea's feelings after the pleasant way she had welcomed her, a stranger into her house.

"Yes, isn't it?" Lukas said. "It's probably just as well you've seen the worst. That way, if we come back here and she shows you her work, you'll be able to make tactful and appropriate comments, without embarrassing yourself or her."

Nadia took a final look at the paintings stacked against the wall.

"Can I get you anything before I head for the shower? You know where the kitchen is. Make yourself at home."

"I wonder if I could use the phone to call my parents. With Gerry's death, you know—they worry." She broke off, swallowing hot tears. "I'll get the time and charges and pay you back." She fought down her grief, looking at the clock on the wall and making a rapid calculation of the time difference. "It must be after eleven there, but I promised I'd call to let them know I'd arrived."

"The phone's in the study downstairs," Lukas told her as he walked toward the door. He paused to stroke a finger down her cheek, noting the quick color that ran up under her skin, the lingering moisture in her dark eyes. "And don't worry about the charges. It's the least I can do after what's happened."

THE CALL WENT THROUGH without incident. The phone at the other end was picked up on the first ring, and before Nadia had a chance to feel surprise, her mother was on the line. Nadia realized at once that Sally was on the verge of hysterics, an unprecedented aberration, given Sally's stiffly formal personality. Not even at the memorial service they'd attended in lieu of a funeral had she shown any emotion other than a couple of controlled, obligatory tears that she had daintily wiped with a lace handkerchief.

"We just received a letter today that was mailed before Gerry's—" Sally stumbled over the word, as if she still hadn't accepted the reality of it. "He found out where Andreas was staying on Atalanti, and like a fool, he was planning to go and see him."

Nadia's mind raced. Andreas Paros was Sally's first husband and Gerry's father. Nadia had never heard the story behind the marriage, only that they had met during a holiday Sally had taken in Greece, and divorced when Gerry was around five. Sally had married again soon after returning to Canada, and a year or so later had given birth to Nadia.

"Is that so bad?" Nadia asked mildly, cutting in on Sally's increasingly shrill declarations.

"Bad?" Sally shrieked. "It could be a disaster. I think Andreas killed him!"

Chapter Four

Nadia felt her face grow pale and cold. Her stomach executed a protesting heave that made her glad it was empty. Sally was not given to exaggeration, which made the apparently wild statement impossible to dismiss out of hand.

"Calm down, Sally. It's been more than thirty years since you left him."

"You've no idea what Andreas was like. The thirst for revenge would burn in him like a disease. He warned me before I left that he'd kill Gerry rather than let me keep him." The tirade became more and more impassioned. "But Gerry was my son too, and I had a right to him, especially since his father never even paid him much attention. He was always going on trips and leaving me alone on that wretched island where nobody spoke any English. You've no idea what it was like."

"But after all this time? Sally, it's not possible."

Nadia heard a muffled gulp as Sally tried to bring herself under control. When she spoke again, her voice was calmer, but tight with an unmistakable undercurrent of fear. "It's possible, believe me. I should never have married Andreas. But I was so young, and that air of danger around him and the idea that my parents would just die if they saw him made me go ahead with it. I soon regretted it, but at least I had Gerry." Her sob was audible and heart-wrenching, all the more so because Sally never cried. "Now he's taken him away. He's won."

"You don't know that, Sally." Nadia attempted to soothe her, knowing it was futile. "But I'll find out."

"Nadia!" Terror shook in Sally's voice. "Come home. Don't push it. He'll get you, too. I tried to phone you earlier today, but they said you'd checked out of your hotel."

"I'm staying with some acquaintances. And don't worry," she said. "The Greek police are on the case and want to find out what happened to Gerry, as you and I do. They don't want the international outrage they'll get if they don't resolve the case."

There. She hoped that calmed her mother.

Still, an involuntary shiver raised goose bumps on her arms. She remembered the car in the narrow street, the blinding glare of headlights, and the suffocating stench of exhaust. Something *was* going on. She squared her shoulders. There was no way she was going to give up now. "I'll give you the phone number where I can be reached."

Sally was not mollified. "It's too dangerous, Nadia. Leave it and come home."

"I can't, Sally," Nadia said as gently as possible. "I have to see it through."

She heard a resigned sigh from her mother. "I might have known. You've got all of your father's stubbornness, and little of his good sense. Do what you must, but don't say I didn't warn you." Her voice rose again. "Andreas is dangerous. Remember that, and be careful."

SHE LOOKED DISTURBED, Lukas thought as he heard her recite the phone number to her party before hanging up. *No, worse.* She looked as if someone had announced another violent death.

"I take it that was your mother," he said, his quiet tone belying his curiosity. "Do you always call her Sally?"

She jumped, as if she hadn't heard his approach. She turned to face him, her eyes bleak. "I have since I was a teenager, at her request." Her abrupt tone told him she was not in the mood for a lengthy explanation.

"Was she upset that you disturbed her this late at night?"

How much had he heard? Not the words, but surely the tone had come through clearly, especially when she had held the receiver away in anguish. "She was waiting up. She phoned the hotel and nearly had a heart attack when she found I wasn't there." She paused for a split second, then added, "I know whom Gerald went to see on Atalanti."

Lukas's mouth dropped open. "What?"

"I said I—"

"I heard what you said," he interrupted. "Whom?"

"His father, Andreas Paros. Except—" she backtracked a bit "—we aren't positive he saw him, only that he was going there about a week before his death.

It's the first I knew that his father was still alive. Sally rarely talked about him."

Lukas paused. "Didn't that strike you as odd?"

Nadia let out a short mocking laugh. "If you knew Sally, you wouldn't ask that question. She has a way of ignoring the unpleasant aspects of life, of blocking them out as if they didn't exist. It couldn't have been much of a love match, because she married again, only months after she returned to Canada and divorced Paros. Within a year I was born, but even from the time I was small I never felt close to her. Oh, she was never cruel or anything, but it was obvious that Gerry was her favorite."

"Didn't you resent it?" He lounged in the doorway, his arms crossed over his chest in a deceptive pose of relaxation. In reality all his senses were alert, the one that warned of possible duplicity clamoring loudest of all. Although what she could be hiding from him, he hadn't a clue.

Nadia shook her head. "Not really, because of the way she was. We were often left with a baby-sitter, so Gerry and I were close. We needed each other. Anyway Sally wasn't the sort who cuddled children, not even Gerry, even though she almost smothered him with sweaters and boots and words of advice."

"The professional mother," Lukas said dryly. "When I hear these stories, I'm glad my mother had a career and allowed—actually expected—us to be independent from an early age." He ran a hand through his hair, combing the thick waves into an unruly disorder that Nadia immediately had an urge to smooth out.

Abruptly she told herself not to be so stupid. Their relationship had to remain strictly business. She'd do well to remember that.

"I think when we get to Epirus, our first order of business will be to go over to that island," Lukas said. "I'd thought of it before, but now I think it's urgent. He must have seen somebody there, to have stayed for several days. And it was the very first night he spent back in the village that he was killed. There has to be a connection."

Placing a hand on her arm, he steered her out of the study. "Come on, time's awasting."

THE STAFF at the Canadian Embassy was no better than the Greek consulate had been in Vancouver. Polite diplomats expressed their condolences and warned her that her mission was foolhardy, that she should leave it up to the police.

"I have their assistance," she repeated, inwardly fuming at their easy buck-passing.

She left them Lukas's house address, and promised to keep them up-to-date regarding any new, dramatic evidence. They had a responsibility to keep tabs on Canadian citizens, and Gerald still rated as one.

Feeling disappointed and filled with trepidation, Nadia then went with Lukas to Gerald's office. It was a ten-minute drive through heavy, but fast-paced traffic, to a modern building just off Sintagma Square in the city center. But when they took the lift to Gerald's floor, only one man was working in E.C.I.'s suite of rooms. The man, Nicholas Mavrakis, added little to their meager store of information, though he had been one of the team that had gone to the quarry that day.

As they settled into leather chairs, Nadia noticed that the lean, tough-looking man appeared ill at ease in his pale summer suit. She'd felt the strength in his hand as he shook hers, the calluses that told her he hadn't spent all his time behind a desk.

"Can you tell me what happened that day?" Nadia asked. She loosened her fingers from their tense grip on the chair arms and clamped them together in her lap.

"We went up to Pefkaki with a team of three men. We inspected the quarry, made suggestions for updating equipment. The foreman in charge said he had no authority to make changes, but if we'd wait a week, we could talk to the owner. In the meantime Gerald went to the island, Atalanti. Said he wanted to see it again and there was no point in wasting the time we had to wait."

"How did he seem when he came back?" Nadia asked. "Disturbed? Agitated?"

Mavrakis shook his head. "No, he seemed as usual."

"What happened that night? Were you with him?"

"No. We were staying in a house at the edge of the village, and he had a room above a coffee shop. He left us, saying he'd meet us at the quarry in the morning."

"Which he didn't do," Lukas put in. He leaned forward, wanting to squeeze Nadia's arm, to comfort her.

"Oh, we found him there all right." Mavrakis swung his rather cold eyes back to Nadia. "We found his body. He was badly beaten, and we had the funeral almost immediately, burying him in the village cemetery. I'm sorry, Miss Roberts. This must be painful for you."

It was, but Nadia's present discomfort came not from the retelling of the details that had been spelled out much more graphically in the police report, but from the uneasy feeling she had that he was not telling her everything. Intuition, perhaps, but the words he spoke rang too glibly, as if he were reciting a tale carefully memorized.

"What made you bury him there, and not in Athens?" she asked with a feeling of futility.

Mavrakis shifted, his chair squeaking. "I was probably his closest friend, Miss Roberts. I knew what was in his will. He didn't want a major production done up for his funeral."

Strange, in a man so young. Why would he have made his wishes about his own death known? Nadia asked herself again. But not entirely surprising, given Gerry's almost Oriental fatalism.

AT THE POLICE STATION Nadia met Lukas's superior, a jowly man whose benign demeanor hid a sharp intelligence and a formidable analytical mind. He was introduced only as Gabriel.

"You're safe with Lukas," he told her with an avuncular chuckle. "He's the best we've got. Your embassy asked for him in particular."

Her brows shot up. "They did? Why didn't they tell me?"

"Because officially they can't get involved. Unofficially they're as anxious to get to the bottom of this as we are."

"And your department," Nadia said. "How do you feel about my involvement?"

"We sympathize with your loss. We don't encourage relatives to go along, but as long as you don't interfere with Lukas's work, what harm can be done?" A frown creased his substantial brow. "Just one caveat: don't go off on your own. It could be dangerous."

A specific warning? Or just a general one? Nadia wondered.

THE SUN, hotter than it had any right to be in April, rode at the zenith of a pure blue sky when they finally burst free of the maze of Athens streets and highway interchanges. On the Corinth motorway, Lukas wove through traffic that to Nadia's North American eyes seemed maniacal in its disregard for common courtesy.

"How far is it?" she asked as they left the city behind.

"To Ioannina, something over four hundred kilometers."

"Five hours' driving?"

Lukas laughed, his eyes twinkling as he glanced at her. "Yeah, if the traffic were light and the road a freeway in Canada. Here it doesn't work that way, I'm afraid. We've got to cross the Corinth Canal west of here and go almost to Patras, take a ferry across the gulf, and continue through Arta up to Ioannina. We'll stop there for the night, and believe me, by then you'll be glad for the break. In the morning we'll motor to the coast and catch whatever transportation they have to the island."

"Isn't there a ferry?"

"Yeah, once a week. This week's went yesterday. The Corfu ferries don't put in there. But we can hire a fisherman to take us over. They're happy to make a little extra on the side."

At the thought of a trip on a small boat, Nadia's stomach rumbled plaintively. Even stepping out onto one of those diabolical floating docks they used at most Vancouver marinas was enough to make her seasick. She could barely stand the ferry ride to Vancouver Island; what would she do on a smelly fishing caïque?

Lukas heard the rumble and misinterpreted it. "We'll stop soon for lunch. There's a good place up ahead."

Forcing a smile to her dry lips, Nadia pushed the thought of sailing aside. She'd worry about it when she was actually on the boat.

"OKAY, TELL ME all about your mother and her ex-husband, since they seem to be figuring rather heavily in this," Lukas said when they were on the road again after an excellent lunch of stewed vegetables and broiled mullet.

"There's not much to tell. This is the first time Sally's ever said anything about her ex-husband other than mentioning his name once when I asked about him, years ago." Nadia frowned, brows knitting together above her nose. "Come to think of it, even then she acted strangely when she spoke of him. Maybe she didn't actually do it, but it was as if she looked over her shoulder to see if he was there. You know how children can sense discomfort in adults."

Lukas grinned. "I suppose."

"Well," Nadia said quickly, "this wasn't embarrassment, it was fear. Something like making a joke about God when you're a kid and wondering if you're going to be struck by lightning."

"Did you make jokes about God, Nadia?" He sounded amused but not as if he was mocking her.

"No, I didn't dare. But Gerald did sometimes." She jumped when a car roared by, skimming their front fender as it overtook them with mere centimeters to spare. "Damn it, are they all idiots once they get behind the wheel?"

"Now, now, Nadia," Lukas chided gently. "Is that any way for a minister's daughter to talk?"

She gaped at him. "How did you know?"

"Know that your father's a minister? When Gerry was killed, we had to check into his background. He'd listed you as next of kin and everything else followed. Let's see now. Soon after she left Greece, your mother met and married your father. Did she know him before? It seems to me it happened awfully fast."

Nadia shook her head. "I don't know. As I said, both our parents were rather distant. They never discussed it."

"Makes you wonder, doesn't it? She'd gone back to her maiden name after the divorce, too, and given it to Gerald as well. That's why we didn't know the identity of her ex-husband. In the light of what you've just said, I suppose she did it out of fear of Andreas Paros."

"Did you find out anything on him? Don't tell me that wasn't what you were doing when you stayed in Gabriel's office after you sent me out into the waiting area?"

He shrugged, a small graceful movement of his shoulders under his light jacket. "I checked out his name, but there's very little on record about him. He's apparently an exemplary citizen, who pays his taxes both here and in England. He has business interests there. What kind is not specified, but I have someone working on it."

"Do you think he's living on the island?"

"According to your mother, it would seem Gerry thought so. The only address we have on him is an office in Athens. We'll find out soon enough."

The miles reeled away beneath them. The wide road hugged the Gulf of Corinth, and they made good time. Fortunately for Nadia's stomach, the narrow strait separating Rion from Antirion was as smooth as glass; she was barely aware of being on a ship at all for the twenty-minute crossing.

"Your mother tried to get you to give this up and come home, didn't she?" Lukas said as they headed north. The hills in the distance were green from the winter rains. A fresh sea breeze carried the scent of wildflowers and thyme to them.

"She thought it might be dangerous." Nadia spoke lightly, her eyes on the passing scenery and a castle shell on a promontory above the plain. At the moment danger seemed far away, Sally's exhortations only a hysterical reaction to the trauma of her son's death.

"How reliable is anything Sally would say? She's not apt to get worked up about nothing, is she?"

"Well, it must be true that Gerry was going to see Andreas, since he wrote of his plans in a letter." She shivered despite the heat. "It must have been quite a shock to receive a letter from someone who was already dead and buried."

"It must have been," Lukas agreed, his eyes warm with sympathy. "But maybe she's overreacting about the danger?"

Nadia gave a firm shake of her head, the sweet scent of her hair drifting to his nostrils as it competed with the perfumes borne on the wind. "If you knew Sally, you wouldn't have to be asking that. She *never* shows emotion. It's not ladylike or refined. Why, she still wears a hat to church on Sunday."

"In a minister's wife, that can't be too odd," Lukas said. "She would have an image to uphold."

"It's not that. She's apparently always been this way, even before she married Father. I don't know how she found herself doing something as wild as marrying someone in a foreign country. In the old photos she showed us, she always looked as if she was dressed for lunch with the Queen."

"No wonder she didn't feel at home among the egalitarian Greeks," Lukas muttered.

"She was so formal, she'd barely allow me to wear jeans when I was a kid. And of course bouncing on the furniture was a capital crime. We weren't allowed to walk on the lawn if it had rained, since that would compact the soil. And it goes without saying that a dandelion wouldn't dare appear on that lawn."

"How'd you manage to break out of the mold?" His look of horror warred with humor.

"What makes you think I have?" In another woman the boldness in her eyes might have been called flirtatious, but in her it was simple directness. She was asking an honest question, to which she expected an honest answer.

For a moment Lukas floundered in indecision. "You were different from what I expected."

"How?" she asked, surprised.

He felt himself blush for the first time in years. "Uh, I guess I expected you to be more formally dressed." He eyed the brightly printed voile skirt she wore with another of her loose shirts, this one in a pale sea blue that picked up a color in the print. "You know, high collars, long sleeves."

"I was wearing long sleeves." Suddenly she laughed, an open sound of complete enjoyment. "Surely you don't expect someone who is in advertising to dress like a nun."

"I didn't know you were in advertising, did I? And I expected Gerry's sister."

"The minister's daughter," she cut in. "Don't you know that ministers' kids are usually the terrors of the town?"

He cast her a quick inquisitive smile before turning his attention back to the road. "Were you?"

She tilted her head to one side, her blue eyes alight with humor. "Yeah, sometimes. When Sally wasn't around."

Where this banter would have led she wasn't to find out, as Lukas glanced into the rearview mirror and frowned. His eyes narrowed against the glare of the sun on a car coming up fast behind them. When it overtook without incident, the tension drained out of his body. "Somebody's in a hurry," he said with seeming nonchalance.

"Like the car that overtook us earlier." She frowned. "Everyone's warning me of danger. How serious do you think it is? And don't give me some pat answer. I want the truth."

"The truth, Nadia?" he said cryptically. "We'll find it, if possible. As for danger, we'll just keep our eyes open." He cast her a direct look, momentarily taking his eyes from the road. "Or would you like to give up and let me go on my way? It's my job, after all."

"No, I'll stick with you. I'm not afraid."

Maybe you should be, he thought, but kept his misgivings to himself. He narrowed his eyes, measuring the bend of the road as he steered the car into it. The tires squealed as he rounded the curve with perfect control. "Tell me something, didn't you ever discuss Gerry's father with either Gerry or your mother?"

"Do you think it's important?"

"Maybe, maybe not. But by his own admission Gerry thought so. He tried to contact him, a man who seems amazingly elusive."

"So you think Sally may be right in thinking that Paros is mixed up in this?"

He shrugged. "Stranger things have happened. On the other hand, maybe Gerry never saw him, or the man is dead or out of the country. It's futile to speculate at this point."

Yes, she could see that. They had only rumors and impressions and the vaguest deductions to go on.

"Gerry was unusually busy these past few years, traveling a lot and writing less often than in the past," she admitted. "We each had our own careers. We lived separate lives. He rarely talked to me about himself whenever he came to Vancouver. And I hadn't seen him for over a year. He was a lot like our mother in personality, controlled and rather formal."

"So you don't know exactly what kind of 'consulting' he did, except that his company specializes in improving industrial efficiency?"

It was becoming apparent that she had allowed the years to distance her too much from Gerry. Too many things had come between them. While in the normal course of events this was to be expected, now she wished she knew more. "No. All I know is that his job involved travel and he used his engineering background."

"So he came to an obscure village to offer services that weren't wanted. And he—and E.C.I.—riled someone."

Nadia sighed under the weight of her own perplexity and powerlessness. "That's what I've been asking myself. What if he upset the entire village and they're hiding the murder? Maybe his death was a warning to the modernizers to stay out."

Lukas nodded. "Could be. We'll just have to find out. Just remember to stick with me. It's unlikely the villagers will threaten an Athens policeman, but you never know. If necessary, I'll call in my backups."

"Why not now?"

He lifted a brow. "We don't want to alert or panic the culprit too soon. So, in the meantime, let's keep a low profile."

Nadia stared at him, taking in the hard line of his profile with its distinctive aquiline nose, the softening effect of his thick lashes. "This is not going to be a simple case, is it?"

"No. Especially after last night. No, I don't think it's simple at all."

A road sign indicated they were nearing Arta, the sign projecting out of a cleft in the rock cliff through which the highway had been carved. Pyramids of gravel lined the road, warning of a construction zone ahead. In the warm late afternoon the sunshine-yellow Renault seemed to be the only vehicle heading north.

At the end of the gorge, barricades equipped with flashing lights appeared beside the heaps of gravel.

"What the hell?" Lukas burst out as a Detour sign painted in emphatic black letters half blocked their lane. "I checked with the highway department and they said the construction was suspended for this week. Nothing about detours."

"Maybe another bridge washout," Nadia suggested, thinking of the road to Pefkaki.

Lukas cast her an impatient look. "Bridges don't wash out on the main road." He braked sharply, stopping the little Renault against the orange barrier that blocked the entire width of the highway. Another Detour sign pointed to a stony track at their right.

He sat for a moment, long fingers tapping the steering wheel. The engine throbbed gently at their backs. Reaching a decision, he put the car into reverse and backed away from the barricade, edging gingerly onto the rough track. "Guess we'll risk it."

"There must be a reason for the sign," Nadia suggested.

"Yes, but it may not be one we like."

The car bumped and lurched over a rutted surface that must have been a quagmire in wet weather. Nadia braced one hand on the dash in front of her, wincing as a rock clanged against the bottom of the vehicle.

Out of sight of the highway the track deteriorated even further, following what appeared to be a dry riverbed before climbing once more toward the crest of a ridge. "We should be able to see Arta once we get to the top."

And a welcome sight it would be. Nadia clutched the armrest with one hand, the dash with the other, her knuckles turning white. From the side window she couldn't see the track at all, only empty space over a checkerboard of cultivated fields far below.

Then it happened. From behind a rock outcropping a green Opel leaped into view, its engine screaming as it careened toward them with deadly intent.

Chapter Five

Lukas, cursing furiously, braked and slammed the transmission into reverse, ignoring the grinding gears. He backed up faster than Nadia had ever seen anyone do, sending Jolie tearing downhill toward a place where the track widened. Such was his speed that he managed to put a space between them and the pursuing automobile.

Making a complicated maneuver involving the clutch, brake and gearshift, he spun the Renault around to face the direction from which they'd just come. For a heart-stopping instant the vehicle seemed suspended above the sheer drop. Nadia sucked in her breath as she felt one of the rear wheels leave the edge of the roadbed. Valiantly the little car recovered, the remaining three wheels gripping tenaciously.

With gravel and dust spurting out from under the spinning tires, Jolie hurtled down the mountain, the Opel inches from her rear bumper.

Their pursuer lost ground in the dry riverbed, but by the time the Renault hit the highway, the Opel was closing fast.

A brightly painted E.L.P.A. truck stood parked just ahead of the detour barrier, the driver standing beside it and scratching his head. Nadia barely had time to register the presence of a witness to the crash that seemed inevitable, when Lukas pulled the wheel hard to the right.

"Hang on!" he shouted.

The car lurched to one side, balancing for an instant on two wheels as it clipped the end of the barrier. The E.L.P.A. man, a startled look on his face, jumped out of the way as the wooden frame fell to the pavement with a clatter. Just in time, too, for an instant later the sound of a sickening crunch told Nadia the Opel had collided with it.

"Are they stopping?" Lukas asked without taking his eyes off the road.

Nadia craned her neck around the headrest. "They're slowing down. The man at the side of the road is shaking his fist." She turned back to Lukas. "What's E.L.P.A.?"

"An organization to help motorists in trouble. He's probably wondering why there's a Detour sign. I seriously suspect our friend in the Opel set us up. How is he doing?"

She looked back again. "Oh, no!" she cried in consternation. "He's coming after us. No damage, I guess, even though he's trashed the barrier."

"Well, then," said Lukas, setting his mouth in a grim line. "I guess we'll have to take some serious evasive action."

"Serious evasive action" involved driving into the outskirts of Arta at a breakneck speed. The Opel kept pace but in the increasing density of the traffic on the road was unable to overtake them.

"Do you know Arta at all?" Nadia asked breathlessly as Lukas in quick succession executed first a right turn, then a left and then another left, before stopping in an alley next to a fenced compound where sun-bleached blocks of marble lay scattered among clumps of weeds fighting for an existence in the dusty ground. The high-pitched scream of a band saw told them someone was busy in the building at the edge of the yard, evidence of an ordinary working day with no hint of vehicular violence.

The adrenaline surging through Nadia's blood dissipated slowly as they waited and nothing happened. She was suddenly seized by a wild trembling that, even when she wrapped her arms around her chest, she could not control.

At once Lukas pulled her against the solid warmth of his body, running a rough but tender hand down the glossy length of her hair. "It's all right," he murmured, one eye on the rearview mirror. "I think we've lost him."

Nadia could feel the sun slanting in through the window of the car, the return of yesterday's headache pounding at her temples. But in Lukas's arms was safety, security. The faintly exotic sandalwood scent of him represented an oasis of normalcy in a world that had suddenly become dangerous.

The band saw whined into silence. Presently the cheerful sound of men calling goodbyes to one another was followed by the roar of starting car engines. A chain clanged against a steel post and the last car accelerated out of the lot, the sound receding slowly. Silence fell over the yard, broken only by a cricket tuning his wings for his nightly serenade.

The street, a dead end where they stood in the shadow of an apparently unused warehouse, lay deserted, dust slowly settling.

Lukas stirred finally, one hand tilting up her chin. "Nadia, you asleep?"

She gave a shaken laugh. "After that wild ride? I may not sleep for a week." She sat up, freeing herself gently from his arms, conscious of relief when he didn't attempt to prolong the embrace. With an effort she pulled herself together, ashamed of her weakness. "Did you ever consider competing at Le Mans?"

His grin flashed. "Yes, as a matter of fact. Once, when I was young and crazy."

She laughed, swallowing as the remnants of her fright threatened again to displace her tightly reined control. "And you're old and sane now?"

He leaned forward to start the engine. "Not so old, not so sane, but I know what I'm doing."

"I'm glad one of us does." She refastened her seat belt, bracing herself as he roared backward out of the alley.

They had just turned in at the main road leading into the center of the town when Nadia called out, "Stop!"

Lukas saw it, too. The green Opel was parked at the curb in front of a service station, its short, stocky driver standing beside the gas pumps, apparently questioning the attendant.

"Okay, that does it," Lukas muttered, his fingers tightening around the steering wheel. "We're going to find out who this guy is and what the hell he thinks he's doing."

Lukas drove the tiny Renault in front of the Opel, backed up against its front bumper and resolutely set the brake. A van double-parked to drop off a delivery effectively blocked the Opel from behind.

"Stay here," Lukas said as he shoved open the door.

But Nadia wasn't one to sit when events were about to erupt. She jumped out on her side, grabbing the keys that he had carelessly left in the ignition.

She answered his black and daunting frown with a sweet smile, dangling the keys in front of his face. "You forgot these."

Snatching them without a word, he strode back to where the Opel's driver, the young service station attendant and the van driver stood frozen like a tableau in a mime play. Lukas, ignoring the others, addressed the stocky man. Nadia could see he was the man who had been in the Plaka taverna last evening. "I'd like a word with you, if I may."

Nadia, with no knowledge of Greek, understood nothing of the words but his attitude was unmistakable.

The stocky man blustered something as he extracted an unfiltered cigarette from a battered pack in his shirt pocket and put it into his mouth, spitting a stray strand of tobacco into the gutter. He struck a match and lighted the cigarette that dangled from his thick lips. Acrid smoke drifted on the still twilight air. Only the faint hissing of a faulty air hose on the wall near the gas pumps disturbed the tense silence.

"Get back from the pumps," Lukas snapped.

Ignoring him, the man blew out smoke, and dropped the match next to an oil spill. It flared momentarily, a little river of fire snaking along the ground. Nadia rushed forward and stamped on the flame. She glared at him, their eyes locking for an instant. The remorseless malevolence in his gaze sliced through her like an icy blade, and she shivered. *See,* he seemed to say, *I've got the upper hand.*

He coolly lit another match, waving it in her face as she stood frozen. "Such a brave lady. It would be a shame to scar that pretty body."

He spoke in rough English.

Lukas pushed past Nadia, anger in every line of his body. He knocked the match out of the man's hand, the flame expiring as it arced harmlessly to the ground.

Nadia sucked in her breath, fighting the sickness that churned in her stomach. The hardness in Lukas's face mirrored his adversary's. For the first time she saw him as he really was, a man as capable of violence as the enemy he faced.

The smell of gasoline on the hot air was thick and cloying. "Move." Lukas lifted his hands threateningly. "You'll blow us sky-high."

The man took a step back, scattering ash as he gestured defiantly. "So? I'll rid the world of one nosy cop."

The comment didn't come as much of a surprise to Lukas. The man's grasp of English did.

"And half a square kilometer of innocent people," Lukas said without the flicker of an eyelid.

The man shrugged, the peculiar pebble-green eyes narrowing against the rising smoke.

Lukas jerked his head toward a coffee shop just up the street. At the same time he pushed his hand inside his jacket, the gesture so quick and seemingly natural that neither of the other men noticed. But Nadia suddenly understood the significance of the hard shape she'd felt when she had laid her arm across his chest in the car.

The man shrugged again, tossing the cigarette butt onto the ground next to a dark stain. Lukas stamped on it, grinding the smoking stub underfoot.

"We'll be right back," Lukas said to the service station attendant, adding a short phrase in Greek. The boy nodded.

Without removing his gaze from the stocky man's face, Lukas took him by the arm and pulled the pack of cigarettes and the matchbook from his pocket and tossed them in the rubbish bin. "Just in case you have any more ideas."

Nadia followed, a little uncertainly. Lukas propelled the man down the street.

The tables outside the coffee shop were set in a courtyard surrounded by a low wall. Lukas pushed the man down onto the cane seat of a chair in the corner, dragging the table in front of him. He planted himself firmly on a chair opposite, as if daring the man to make an escape.

Nadia sank down next to Lukas, her hands sweating as she tensely gripped the shoulder strap of her purse.

A waiter came running, and Lukas abruptly ordered three coffees before gesturing the man away.

He fixed his captive with a menacing stare that chilled the pit of Nadia's stomach more effectively than the thought of going onto a boat had ever done. "Okay, my man, let's have it. We'll start with your name."

Oddly the man didn't appear reluctant to reveal his name. For an instant Nadia wondered if he was lying, but decided she was being fanciful. "Kyriakos Halias," the man announced with a pride that rang of truth.

"Okay, Kyriakos Halias, why are you following us, and why did you try to run us off the road? Not to mention last night's little encounter on a street restricted to pedestrian traffic. That was you, wasn't it?"

Halias's broad jaw set pugnaciously, and he allowed himself an evil smile, revealing stained and chipped teeth. A cuspid was missing, obviously the victim of some long-ago brawl. Nadia wondered if the man was armed and what would happen if he decided to fight his way out of where Lukas had cornered him.

The question was partially answered when Halias stealthily shifted his hands toward the edge of the table. At once Lukas snapped, "Keep your hands on the table, where I can see them."

Lukas didn't think the man had a gun. Otherwise he would have been shooting at them earlier. But a knife—*yes.* Mr. Halias looked the sort to carry a deadly switchblade in his pocket or a larger knife strapped to his ankle. With a razor-edged blade either could, at close range, kill as swiftly and surely as a bullet.

He glanced at Nadia, soaking in the frightened tension he could see in her face. He also noticed the resolute lines that spoke of courage and determination.

He was about to say something when the coffee came. None of them made any pretense of drinking it. Nadia gulped down the water from one of the glasses the waiter also set on the table, wrapping her hand around the chilled condensation on the outside of the glass as if it were a talisman against the fear churning inside her.

"Who are you working for?" Lukas began, knowing he wouldn't get an honest answer.

The stocky man tilted his head back on his thick neck and laughed uproariously. "Surely you don't think I'd tell you, do you, cop?"

"Okay." Lukas inclined his head. "Then let me tell you what I already know. Judging from the idioms you use, you've spent some time in North America." He looked at the man. "How'm I doing so far?"

The man's smile slipped.

"And," Lukas went on, "I'd guess you've spent a good many years in the Middle East, as well. I thought I heard some Arabic in your comment at the gas station."

The man struggled to get up, cursing in a guttural accent. Lukas slammed the table back against him. The swearing stopped abruptly in a grunt of pain, as the edge of the table caught him under the diaphragm.

Lukas, feeling slightly sick to his stomach, knew it was useless. This was a tough customer, trained as a killer for hire, who took human life with less remorse than a normal person felt after swatting a mosquito. To get real information from him would require tactics not even Devil's Island would condone, never mind an innocuous Arta coffee shop.

Lukas stood up, ignoring the black coffee thickening to mud in the tiny cups. Taking Nadia's arm in his, the hostile gaze he fixed upon his erstwhile prisoner never wavering, he pulled her up. "Come on, Nadia. Let's go."

"But aren't you—" She stumbled as he dragged her away from the table. On the way to the street, he tossed a handful of coins to the waiter, who expertly caught them in one hand.

"Nadia, let's not discuss anything here."

Gasping, his heavy jowls livid, Halias swore again. "I know what you're after, and I can tell you, you won't get it."

Lukas paused, turning to face the man. "Won't I? We'll see if people like you and whoever you're working for can kill innocent people with impunity."

A crafty smile transformed Halias's broad face. "Who's the judge of innocence or guilt?"

They were almost at the entrance to the courtyard when Halias made his final threat. "Give it up, or you'll end up like your friend—dead."

Chapter Six

Night had fallen by the time Lukas and Nadia reached Ioannina. To Nadia's eyes the city appeared old, its streets meandering without plan, as though pavement had been laid on top of widened goat trails. To their left the lights of scattered villages lay like winking jewels on the surrounding mountains. At the right, the lake stretched dark and mysterious, brooding under a pale night mist. Near shore the city's lights were reflected in the glassy surface.

Lukas took them to a hotel in the center of the city, close to a park filled with towering trees and the sound of running water.

Nadia shivered in the chill air, as she got out of the car, wrapping her arms around her chest and wishing she hadn't packed her sweater in her suitcase. She smiled wanly as Lukas pulled off his jacket and offered it to her.

"But you'll be cold."

"I'll be okay." His tone was abrupt, not matching the courtesy with which he held the collar so that she could push her arms into the sleeves.

The jacket enveloped her, the scent of it so evocative of its owner that further protest died in her throat. She briefly closed her eyes, snuggling into the warmth, grateful for the indefinable sense of reassurance it gave her.

"Let's get this stuff into the hotel."

Her eyes shot open. His mouth was set in a taut line without a hint of softness. Since the incident with Halias, he had changed. There had been no more bantering conversations and sly humor. He'd resumed the role of a policeman who concentrated all his energies on the case.

She took hold of her suitcase and marched up the steps of the hotel into the lobby.

Their rooms were adjacent but not connected to each other. At the door, Nadia set down her case and shrugged out of Lukas's jacket. He took it wordlessly, slinging it over his shoulder and gazing at her. "Can you be ready in half an hour?" he asked, his voice gentle this time. "We'll go and get something to eat."

Overwhelmed by the adventures of the day, Nadia wanted nothing more than to be alone. "Couldn't I call room service? I'm tired."

Lukas shook his head. "This isn't the Hilton. There is no room service."

His eyes were soft, liquid as amber honey. She couldn't resist their appeal. "Okay, then." She spoke offhandedly, determined to keep her wits about her, especially when he turned on that easy charm. "I'll be ready in thirty minutes."

The room contained only a sink. As the desk clerk had advised, the shower and toilet were located down the hall. Nadia made do with a quick wash, promising herself a shower later on, then changed into corduroy jeans and a thick woolen sweater. She brushed her hair, and was out in the hall waiting when Lukas emerged from his room.

IN TRUTH Lukas had spent very little time freshening up, and he hadn't bothered to change, except to pull on a sweater over his shirt. He had placed his case in his room and had immediately gone out again in search of the local O.T.E. office. Reaching it a scant minute before closing time, he had been forced to use his police badge to persuade the man on duty to put through a call to Gabriel. But in the end it had been useless. Nothing had turned up on Andreas Paros, nor was there any information on a Kyriakos Halias.

He had spent the remainder of the half hour pacing his room, trying to make some sense of the situation.

If Gerald Parker's death was a simple case of murder by disgruntled workers in the marble quarry, or by an angry village father for real or imagined wrongs done to a daughter, why was a professional hit man following them? What was worse, he was either trying to kill them or scare them away.

Lukas could only hope his department turned up something on Halias and Paros soon. Events were not shaping up well at all. But if they deteriorated too quickly, Lukas would just call in his backup team ahead of schedule—if he could reach a phone in time.

He stepped out of his room and found Nadia in the hall, her expression a little uncertain. He suppressed a shiver of dread. What had he brought her into?

She had come to Greece to solve her brother's murder, a worthy objective. Courage and loyalty were keeping her fixed on her goal. He admired those qualities in her; in fact they had made the attraction between them stronger. But that admirable and occasionally reckless determination might yet get her into trouble. He wasn't sure he'd be able to protect her then. It would be safer for both of them if she left.

But short of hustling her bodily onto a plane and out of the country, what could he do?

Besides, deep down inside, didn't he want her to stay? If only he could keep her out of danger until this was over.

THEY ATE DINNER on a balcony overlooking the lake. The evening was cool, but overhead heaters took the chill from the air. Around them couples and families sat at the other tables, the sounds of dining, conversation and children's laughter creating an illusion that this was just an ordinary dinner date.

Lukas at first kept an eye on the door, waiting for some sign that the driver of the green Opel had arrived. Gradually, as the food filled the empty space in his stomach and the wine he drank sparingly warmed his blood, he allowed himself to relax.

"D'you think that guy Halias or whatever his name is knows where we are?" Nadia asked.

Lukas tipped back his chair, his fingers toying with his wineglass. "Probably. He struck me as the thorough sort."

Nadia frowned, laying her fork and knife across her plate with a clatter. "What are you going to do about it?"

He shrugged. "Not much. There's nothing solid I can arrest him on. We'll keep our eyes peeled tomorrow."

The flickering candle on the table was reflected in his eyes, giving them a lambent glow, as if he could see in the dark. Nadia stared at him. "You don't seem worried."

"What good would it do? Time enough to worry when he tries his next shot at us. And this time we'll be prepared."

"You're carrying a gun, aren't you?"

He neither confirmed nor denied it. Instead he laid his hand over hers on the table. "Nadia, let me handle it, okay? The fact is, I don't like this situation at all. I'd much rather you went back to Athens and let me go on from here alone, but I don't suppose you'd agree to that, would you?"

"You suppose right," she said flatly. "I can't go back. Gerald was my brother. I have to find out what happened to him."

Her fingers felt icy under his. He rubbed them gently, pleased when she didn't free them. "Finding out won't bring him back, you know."

Her full lower lip trembled. "I know. But Lukas, I have to do this."

He smiled. "That's the only reason I'm letting you stay. I understand how I'd feel if it was me."

They walked back to the hotel under a moon that sailed high in the sky and gave the night a white radiance almost as bright as day. *A night made for lovers,* Lukas thought, immediately chiding himself for the romantic fantasy.

Nadia strode silently beside him, independent, withdrawn, her arms swinging freely. He didn't blame her. He had been abrupt with her when they'd checked into the hotel, and he hadn't helped matters by revealing his resistance to her presence. On an intellectual level he understood her need to withdraw, but he found it impossible to suppress his instinct to protect her. And that distraction from complete concentration on the investigation might prove fatal for both of them.

Oh, he knew that Halias was just playing. For now. But if there was more to this than a simple crime of passion or honor, things could get rough fast. And he'd rather he didn't have Nadia in the line of fire.

Besides, the chemistry between them was dulling the edge of his perception, which might just give Halias the second he needed for an advantage the next time he struck.

A sharp explosion shattered the stillness. Lukas grabbed Nadia around the waist and almost threw her into a recessed doorway, his heart pounding in his throat.

A shot? The gun he carried, small and flat, rested under his armpit, hidden by the loose fit of his sweater. He snaked a hand under the hem, grasping the butt as his eyes traveled up and down the narrow street.

Beside him Nadia made a sound. He realized he'd pushed her up against the doorjamb. Releasing his hold slightly, he cautioned her with his eyes to remain silent.

Nothing moved on the street. A couple, hand in hand, strolled by, the whisper of a kiss carrying in the silence. Lukas waited until they had passed, then leaned out of the doorway. He felt the soft pressure of Nadia's breasts against his back as she peered around him.

Headlights flashed on. Nadia started as if she'd been touched by a live wire, and he knew she was remembering last night in Athens.

He drew the gun, holding it ready as the car, its engine silent, rolled down the cobbled street toward them. But his precautions proved unnecessary. As it came abreast, the car gave a spasmodic jerk, and the engine caught, emitting a loud backfire.

"Damn, that's what it was," Nadia said, her voice ripe with self-derision. "This thing has really got us going, jumping at sounds and shadows."

Lukas jammed the gun back into its holster. "Better to be safe than sorry."

"I guess." She sounded more angry than scared. "Ouch."

"Sorry. Did I hurt you?"

"No, I just bumped the place I hurt last night." She gave him a smile that looked somewhat forced. "Thanks. Again. You seem to be making a habit of pushing me out of the paths of cars."

"My job," he said. "That's why you should be staying in Athens and waiting for me. It would be easier to do my job, only having my own skin to worry about."

No more incidents disturbed the quiet streets as they continued to the hotel. If Halias was in the neighborhood, he was lying low.

Lukas unlocked the door of Nadia's room. Gesturing for her to wait outside, he entered first, checking in the old-fashioned wardrobe and under the bed. Nothing. No sign of disturbance.

He came back to the door, swinging it wide open. "It's okay."

"Thanks," she said on a note of irony. "Nothing bigger than a midget could hide in here."

"So call me paranoid. Remember it's—"

"I know." She sighed wearily. "It's your job." She didn't know why she felt so dispirited. Probably still jet lag.

She sensed his sympathy as he hesitated by the door, his eyes gazing into hers. She stood still, fascinated by the golden color that seemed to change in the dim light of the hall. His chest rose and fell as he exhaled deeply. Lifting one hand, he gently touched her face and stroked a finger down her jaw. His warm breath, sweetly wine-scented, drifted over her mouth in a whisper that was not quite a kiss.

"Good night, Nadia. Sleep well."

Which was exactly what she didn't do, for several hours.

Too keyed up to relax, she lay in her bed, listening to the plaintive melody of Lukas's flute drifting faintly through the wall that separated their rooms. At last she went to sleep, the melancholy notes singing in her dreams.

"COME ON, NADIA, you can easily jump that. And I'll catch you, don't worry."

Nadia looked at the rocking deck of the green caïque and the concrete dock on which she stood. A meter's length of black water yawned between them. Luckily her breakfast of fresh bread and aromatic mountain honey had been eaten hours ago, so she couldn't get ill. But now, with the noon sun beating on her head and her feet seemingly glued to a dock in Igoumenitsa, she wished she'd had something more memorable for her last meal. *We who are about to die salute you.* The rallying cry of the gladiators rang absurdly through her head.

"Nadia," Lukas called again, feet apart as he expertly balanced himself on the bobbing boat, "you can do it."

"I can make the jump," she said faintly. "But I can't—I just can't get on that boat."

"What?" he said in patent disbelief. Then a slow smile of comprehension slid over his face, and he laughed with unholy glee.

Lithely he vaulted the strip of water, landing on tiptoe beside her. "And here I thought you were Superwoman. Why didn't you tell me you get seasick?"

"Because then you would have left me behind," she wailed plaintively.

He cocked his head, scratching absently at a spot on his temple that a mosquito had bitten last night. *Yeah,* maybe he would have, since it would have lent additional weight to his reluctance to have her, an untrained civilian, accompany him into danger. "No, I wouldn't have," he lied stoutly. "I would have done what we're going to do now."

With a word to the amused fisherman who waited patiently by, he took Nadia's arm and led her down the street to a pharmacy. There he purchased a small bottle of pink tablets, giving her two immediately with a glass of water offered by an understanding pharmacist.

"They're fast working. By the time we get out of the harbor, you won't even be aware of the boat."

"Oh, yeah?" she muttered skeptically.

But it was true. After a slight initial queasiness, her stomach settled down. As the boat put out into the open sea, Nadia found she could even enjoy the sensation of motion and the freshness of the breeze playing across the deck. She even laughed at the antics of a pair of dolphins who cavorted in front of the bow.

She could also enjoy the sight of Lukas, shirtless despite the sometimes biting wind gusting from snow-capped mountains that lined the shore. His body was bronzed, and his broad chest was matted with black hair that narrowed to a triangle at his trim waist. His pale blue jeans rode low on his lean hips, enhancing his strong muscles. He lounged in a tipped-back chair beside the fisherman. To judge by the constant hand gestures and loud bursts of laughter, they were already fast friends.

Nadia fought a faint jealousy, then recognized it as loneliness. Because of the language barrier she was excluded from the conversation. Banishing the feeling as petty and childish, she lay back in the comfortably padded seat the fisherman had provided for her, and gave herself up to the warmth of the sun.

Her mind raced as she wondered what they would find on the island. Andreas Paros, Gerry's father? Since Nadia's father had raised him from the age of five, Nadia couldn't picture Gerry and the mysterious Andreas together. Despite his threats, Andreas hadn't stormed over to Canada to take possession of his son.

Why hadn't he? Was Sally exaggerating his anger? If he was a successful businessman as Lukas had indicated, he would have had the means not only to locate Sally but to force her to give up her son. He hadn't done so.

It was a puzzle, but perhaps not as great a one as the questions of whether Gerry had actually seen him, and whether the visit had led to Gerry's death. Nadia shook her head. Despite Sally's hysteria, she couldn't believe Andreas would have carried out his threat after some thirty years. No matter how possessive he might have felt toward a child, surely he knew he had no power over the adult Gerry.

No. It had to be something else, something they were overlooking.

Squinting her eyes against the sun that flashed light off the newly formed whitecaps, she scanned the distant horizon. A white form, towing a banner of foam, turned out to be the Corfu ferry. Its wide decks were virtually deserted as it headed for the mainland. Their sturdy caïque rocked as the ferry's wake reached them.

A thump of sneaker-shod feet and an altered rhythm in the sway of the boat announced Lukas's presence next to her. He plopped onto the seat beside her, throwing one arm casually along her shoulders and cradling her face against his bare chest.

His skin was cool under her cheek, the hairs tickling her nose. As the fisherman corrected their course, rolling the boat to the left, Nadia put up a hand to brace herself. Her fingers tangled in the mat of hair on Lukas's chest. She could not resist curling them toward her suddenly damp palm.

The hair was soft, and at the same time crisp. It was resilient, shining with an iridescent glossiness under the sun. Slowly she loosened her hold, spreading her hand flat against his skin. She could feel the heavy beat of his heart under her palm, an elemental pulse that began to stir a complementary rhythm in her own body.

The tenderness in his eyes as she brought hers up to meet them was a surprise after his almost brotherly treatment of her seasickness.

But then the fisherman's bellow shattered the quiet. "Atalanti!" Nadia scrambled up awkwardly, peering at the last place that her brother had visited before his death.

NADIA DISEMBARKED in silence, carrying her suitcase and assiduously avoiding Lukas's eyes. When he stood on the jetty beside her, she realized it wasn't necessary. He wasn't looking at her, either.

It was insane. Her face flaming, she couldn't deny that for a moment her only thought had been of how it would feel to have his hardness against her, to feel sweet rapture in his arms.

Even with Dorian she'd never been so wanton, and she'd known him a year before they made love.

Lukas she didn't know at all, and she had to be out of her mind to think of making love with him. As for a relationship, that was completely out of the question. She'd be crazy to ignore the lesson she'd learned with Dorian. She needed another Greek lover like she needed an attack of the plague. Her head told her all these things, rang with warnings.

But her heart had other ideas, especially when she heard Lukas's husky voice, saw the genuine caring in his eyes.

He took her arm, before she could erect any barriers against him. Her heart lay undefended, a treasure for him to plunder, if he only knew it.

Apparently he didn't, for he merely steered her toward the end of the jetty.

The village was a bare hundred meters long, stretching in a row of weather-beaten stone buildings. They needed a fresh coat of whitewash. Half the windows were boarded up, and others were broken, staring like vacant eyes at Nadia and Lukas.

Two old women dressed in unrelieved black, stopped to stare at the visitors. One, pulling at the folds of her head scarf, muttered something and crossed herself. The other only stared, her black eyes glittering. Nadia shivered, glad of Lukas's presence as an interpreter.

Lukas frowned. While the islanders might lead an insular existence he hadn't expected this hostility, an attitude that certainly wasn't typical. Something was very wrong here. As soon as possible he had to put in another call to Athens.

But first they had to find Andreas Paros.

"*Herete,*" he greeted the two women.

Their eyes never wavered.

He tried again. "*Kalispera.* Good afternoon."

Nothing.

A shout behind them made Lukas and Nadia spin around. They saw a man loping toward them from the edge of the village, his white hair a beacon in the suddenly cloudy afternoon. As though released by an unseen signal the women turned and scuttled down the street, moving faster than anyone would have thought possible at their age.

"Herete," the man greeted them, his face neither hostile nor welcoming.

"Herete," Lukas replied, inclining his head politely.

The man ignored Nadia after staring for a long moment at her hair. The wind on the boat had churned the tawny curls into disorder. The astonished fascination in his gaze faded as he stopped in front of them.

"What do you want here?" the man asked Lukas, his Greek oddly accented, his tone bordering on belligerence. "We have no tourist sights, no hotels."

"We've come to see Andreas Paros."

Lukas had been closely gauging the other man's reaction to the name, but was completely unprepared when his face twisted into a mask of such hate and pent-up fury that Lukas tensed for an attack.

The man contented himself by spitting into the dust an inch from the toe of Lukas's sneaker. Squaring his narrow shoulders, he stretched to his full height and peered into Lukas's eyes.

"Andreas Paros?" Saliva flecked the man's pale lips, and his voice dripped with venom. "He's dead. He's been dead for forty years."

Chapter Seven

"What did he say?" Nadia was panting as she ran to keep up with Lukas's long strides. Like someone suddenly gone crazy, he had turned away from the white-haired man and headed for the far end of the row of buildings.

He looked neither to the left nor the right. "He said that Andreas Paros has been dead for forty years."

"What?" She stopped in her tracks, her mouth falling open. "Was Gerry mistaken, then? He must have had reason to believe his father was here. It's not as if this place is on one of the main tourist routes."

"Katára," Lukas said succinctly. He kept on walking, and again she had to run to catch up.

"What? What's this *katára*?"

"It's a curse. The recipient of it is considered dead. I don't think Paros is physically dead at all. But to the villagers, he'd dead. It's a form of ostracism."

"That's cruel."

"Yes, it is," he agreed. "Greeks must be among the most gregarious people in the world. To exclude someone from all social interaction is a desperate act. Paros must have done something abominable."

"But forty years. Don't they ever forgive?"

"No. Not if it's serious."

The harshness in his voice turned Nadia's stomach to ice. Even the sun emerging from the clouds failed to warm her as she followed the rocky track. It was just what her mother had warned her about.

No wonder she and Dorian had always been at odds. They'd argued from different views of life.

And now, almost as if bewitched, she was repeating history by falling for a man even closer to his heritage than Dorian had been. Even now he might be digging up reasons to justify Gerald's death.

She didn't realize Lukas had stopped until she bumped into him, the impact knocking her suitcase out of her hand.

"Why are you looking at me like that?"

"Like what?" Knowing her face must have given her away, she tried to bluff.

"Like you picked up what you thought was an eel and realized it was a venomous snake."

She bent to retrieve her suitcase, rubbing her thumb on the scuff caused by its hard landing on a boulder next to the path. "Maybe I have."

He made a sound that could have been a laugh. "Me? Come on, Nadia. Me? I'm one of the good guys, remember?"

"Are any of you really good guys?"

He frowned and she saw the beginnings of anger come into his eyes. "Any of who? Policemen? Greeks?"

She sighed. Maybe she was being judgmental. The momentary silence was filled with the sound of pebbles rolling under their feet and twigs snapping.

"Okay. You got me. I apologize. Where the hell are we going, anyway? This path doesn't go anywhere."

"Yes, it does. It must go somewhere. It's the only path. This island isn't very big."

"I've noticed," she said, barely checking her exasperation.

He regarded her narrowly for a moment. "I meant to tell you earlier—Gerry took the same boat we did. That fisherman does good business by making quick trips from the mainland to the island and back. He remembered Gerry well, said he asked about Paros. The fisherman told him to inquire at a monastery on the other side of the island, since the villagers here don't take kindly to strangers. They've been mistrustful since the war."

Nadia's irritation drained away. "Did he find Paros? That's the question we have to answer. Unless the man is really dead."

"I don't think he is. There would be a record of it in Athens if he were. He's a Greek citizen." He frowned. "The fisherman said Gerry seemed in an odd mood on the return trip. He didn't talk much, but he mentioned that an earthquake a number of years ago had done more damage in the interior of the island than on the coast."

Nadia seized eagerly on this piece of information. "Maybe that explains it."

"Explains what?"

"Why Paros isn't here."

"But we don't know that."

"We can assume it." She grasped his forearm, her eyes imploring. "Gerry only stayed a few days. If he'd found his father, wouldn't he have stayed longer?"

"Depends what reception he got." In spite of everything, Lukas began to look intrigued, a smile tugging at his mouth.

"But," Nadia declared, "it's more likely that he didn't find Paros here—that Paros had left the island because of the earthquake. We should be looking for his house. It was a good size, and some distance from the village, according to Sally. She said it was isolated."

"Well, we should find it soon, if it exists. Or the monastery, which may be a better bet. We're nearly at the top of the ridge. We'll be able to see most of the island from there."

The hill's crest was hardly Mount Olympus, but it did provide a perch from which they could view the entire island. A misty coastline stretched to the north-east.

"That's Albania over there," Lukas said, his eyes narrowed as he scanned the rocky, shrub-studded landscape around them. The high-pitched bleat of sheep drifted on the breeze, pulling his gaze to the right. A green patch halfway down a ravine indicated the presence of water. But the sudden bark of a dog from a makeshift sheep pen was a signal that they might be wise to keep a safe distance.

A tall figure wearing a black cloak emerged from a stone hut that blended into the hillside as if it were part of the terrain. He stood with a shepherd's crook in hand, staring up the hill. A dog that looked no more domesticated than a jackal circled him with a feral slinking walk.

Nadia looked at Lukas. "Would he give us directions, do you think?"

"More likely send his dog after us. Do you want to take the risk?"

"No, I guess not. That dog looks part wolf."

"He probably is," Lukas agreed. He noted a faint path leading down the hill in the opposite direction to the shepherd's camp. "I think we'll try that one, and hope we find some place to stay before it gets dark."

The sun was fading fast as it moved toward a cloud bank massing in the west. After dark it would be cold out in the open, Nadia knew, remembering Ioannina last night.

"Why didn't we just look for a place to stay in the village?" she asked as they resumed their trek. Hunger gnawed at her stomach, reminding her that neither of them had eaten since breakfast.

"The impression I got was that they would have locked their doors in our faces and hidden their children under the beds."

"I didn't see any children."

"Exactly. There are no children, nor any adults under the age of forty."

"We only saw three adults," she reminded him. "How do you know who else is there?"

"Because I know a bit about history. I think it's safe to say this island suffered heavily during the civil war around 1948. All over Epirus, children were taken from the villages and marched or driven to Communist countries. I think that's what happened here. All the children were taken off the island, and now, almost forty years later, there are only old people."

"Forty years." Nadia stopped and looked at him in horror. "Do you suppose Andreas Paros—"

"Yes, I do suppose he had a hand in it," Lukas said grimly. "Unless he betrayed his countrymen to the Nazis. But I doubt very much that the Germans would have been interested in an island whose only products are sheep and rocks. So it had to be the civil war."

Nadia digested this in silence. "Greece has had a turbulent history, hasn't it?"

Lukas's eyes dimmed. He shrugged in a gesture that Nadia recognized as purely Greek, an almost fatalistic acceptance of what was unchangeable. "*Te na kaneme?* What can we do?"

"Fight," Nadia said.

He looked at her, his eyes widening in amazement as a slow smile crept over his face. "That's what we've done, as best we could. But I should have guessed you'd suggest it."

"Sometimes it's necessary," she said, scattering pebbles with her feet as she started off down the path again. "And I'd certainly like to know exactly what Gerry got himself mixed up in. It gets more and more complicated, doesn't it?"

"Let's say," he said, falling into step beside her, "it's not getting easier."

They crested another ridge, which ended in a sharp drop to the sea. The rhythmic sound of breakers against the rocks traveled up the hill, dulled by distance but remaining as menacing as ever. Heavy gray clouds hid the sun, casting a pall over the desolate hilltop. Twilight had arrived.

Nadia shivered, more from nerves than from the cold, she thought. This place was spooky, silent except for the sea and the wind rattling dry thorn bushes.

Even the shepherd they'd seen might have been a figment of their imagination.

"I don't know," Lukas muttered as they stopped for a moment in a grove of stunted oaks. Around some of the trunks wound what looked to Nadia like the thorny stems of roses. The buds were swollen to bursting, some showing the color of the blossoms.

"Lukas, look, aren't those Peace roses?"

He examined the gold-tipped buds. "Sure looks like it." Stepping forward, he scanned the grove. Ahead of them, the gloom lightened. They entered a clearing choked with shrubs gone wild, and bordered by a ragged boxwood hedge. "An old garden?" Nadia asked, chewing on her lower lip. "Do you suppose this is where Paros used to live?"

"It's possible," Lukas agreed. "But there's nothing here now, not even the elusive monastery. It looks like a path to nowhere. And I think we're in for a drenching."

They were about to turn back and risk the dubious hospitality of the shepherd's camp, when the harsh clang of a bell brought them up short.

"That sounds like a church bell," Nadia exclaimed. "Could it be the monastery?"

"Must be. Come on, let's go down. Bells don't ring by themselves."

Don't they? Nadia smiled to herself. Anything seemed possible here. Within minutes, they broke through a dense thicket and faced a wrought iron gate that hung by a single hinge. The building beyond sprawled out low and rambling. Built of gray granite, it appeared deserted. Only the swaying of the frayed rope that hung from the detached bell tower pointed to a possible human presence.

Nadia followed Lukas up the flagstone path to a massive wooden door framed by overgrown weeds. He rapped the brass knocker in the form of a gargoyle. The heavy thud echoed over the roar of the sea a hundred feet below the cliff on which the monastery stood.

The shuffle of feet and the tap of a cane preceded the ominous creak of the door as it opened. An old man peered out, his face framed in gray hair that had the texture of Spanish moss. His beard, scraggly and unkempt, hung over a rusty black robe.

Nadia understood nothing of the exchange that followed, but when Lukas turned and took the suitcase from her, she knew they'd been granted shelter for the night.

The building was run-down. It appeared to have suffered extensive damage in the earthquake. Nadia wondered how long ago that had been, since she hadn't heard of any recent seismic disturbances in northwestern Greece.

Many of the rooms they passed as they followed the monk down one corridor after another were heaped with rubble and open to the sky. As they walked, dust balls scattered and shadows lurked in every corner. Nadia felt as if she'd been transported back in time to the Middle Ages; she wouldn't have been surprised if a knight in armor had come clanking toward them.

Where was the monk taking them? They must have circled the entire building by now. She glanced at Lukas. He didn't seem worried as he shortened his stride to keep pace with the monk's shuffling gait.

Something scuttled out from under her feet and she stifled an involuntary cry. A gecko, the innocuous lizard she knew was common in Greece, climbed the wall next to her, pausing to stare with unblinking eyes. Then, with a flick of its long tail, it vanished into a crack between the stones, frightened by a huge orange cat that appeared on silent feet around the curve of the passageway. Nadia suppressed a shudder as she saw the rat, still twitching, clamped firmly between its teeth.

They came to a Spartan room furnished with two narrow cots, a straight-backed cane chair, and a marble-topped washstand sporting a pitcher and basin. With a softly spoken word to Lukas the monk left them, the scuffing of his sandals a gentle counterpoint to the tap of his cane down the hall.

Lukas glanced around the room. "I guess this is home for the night."

The cot sagged under her weight as Nadia sat on its edge. "This has been nothing but a wild-goose chase, hasn't it?" Despite her excellent physical condition, she was tired after the hike over difficult terrain, and depressed that they hadn't located Paros's house before twilight.

"Don't give up so soon, Nadia. Even if Andreas Paros isn't on the island, someone may know where he went, or what happened to him. And we haven't even been to Pefkaki yet. The answers may all be hidden there."

"Probably another dead end. This place is creepy. Did you see the size of that rat the cat had?" She shuddered.

"That's his job, to catch them." The springs of the second cot groaned as Lukas sank into it, testing its ability to hold his weight. "It'll be okay, Nadia. We've only just started." He gave her a warm smile, then got to his feet again. "If you want to freshen up, the monk said there's a toilet just down the hall. I don't know what condition you'll find it in." He lifted the pitcher. "I'll get us some water."

The little room down the hall was immaculate, though the fixtures were strange to Nadia. Obviously the monk, despite his age and isolation, kept to certain standards of housekeeping. The bedroom he'd given them was also meticulously clean.

She returned to it and found Lukas drying his face on a rough towel. He took the basin of used water over to the window and dumped it out. "Should you?" Nadia asked. "What if there's somebody down there?"

"Not likely," Lukas drawled. "Take a look."

She leaned out, and nearly cracked her head on the window frame as she jerked back from the sight. Below them a sheer cliff cascaded to the sea which smashed relentlessly against the rocks, as if it were a beast intent on devouring the island.

Nadia washed her face and hands, using a mirror from her purse to help her restore order to her tangled hair. Sweeping it back from her face, she secured the ponytail with an elastic band. Her eyes were enormous in her pale face. She scowled at her reflection and snapped the compact shut.

Lukas's eyes were on her when she turned, but he said nothing, merely tucking a stray lock of hair behind her ear before leading the way into the hall.

The medieval kitchen was where the monk cooked and ate and probably spent most of his time. Next to the smoldering hearth the cat sat washing himself, having apparently dined well.

They conversed casually over a true peasant meal, consisting of thick lentil soup and a salad of boiled greens, dressed with lemon juice and olive oil and pleasantly bitter.

To her surprise Nadia found that Father Sotiris spoke passable French, a language she knew well. Since it was also one of Lukas's languages, communication was greatly simplified.

After they had eaten, Father Sotiris stacked the dishes in the marble sink, and they pulled their chairs into a circle around the fire. The cat, after a momentary hesitation, jumped onto Nadia's lap, where he settled himself and purred.

"You've come seeking Andreas Paros," the monk said, his eyes on the fire rather than on them. "You're not the first to do so. Some days ago—" he uttered a laugh that sounded rough and unused "—one loses track of time here—a man, a Canadian, I believe he said he was, came here, also asking about Paros."

"He was my brother," Nadia said, leaning forward eagerly, sinking her fingers into the dense plush of the cat's fur.

Lukas tipped back his chair and lifted his feet onto the raised hearth. "In the village they said Paros has been dead for forty years."

"It's the curse." Father Sotiris turned to Nadia. "Do you understand about the curse, madame?"

She nodded. "Lukas explained it to me."

The monk inclined his head. "To the villagers he's dead, but in fact he's very much alive, although he rarely comes here anymore. His house was badly damaged in an earthquake, and the villagers, who had a kind of superstition about coming near Andreas, took it as a sign and completed the destruction while he was away on one of his trips. There's not a single brick of it left."

"Except the remains of the garden," Nadia said. "Was it in a grove of oaks near here?"

"Yes. He liked his privacy. It was hard on his wife, though. She left years ago."

"Is Andreas living in Pefkaki, on the mainland?" Lukas asked.

"Some of the time. When he's not in London or Paris or New York. Our Monsieur Paros had done well for himself since he was a fisherman's son on Atalanti."

"In what line of business?" Lukas had Gabriel in the Athens police department working on the answer to that question, but if the monk told him he wouldn't have to wait.

No answer was forthcoming, however. The old man might not have heard the question. "The villagers put a curse on Andreas Paros when they found out that he was behind the kidnapping of their children. The children were taken out at night, put onto boats and ferried across to Albania. Some of their parents were Communist sympathizers, of course, and sent their children willingly. They thought their children would get a better education and have greater opportunities than was possible on this island. But other children were simply taken away."

"Couldn't anyone stop it?" Nadia felt sick with horror.

The monk shook his head, his black eyes glittering in the firelight. "The country was in chaos, still recovering from the war. Then this civil war broke out, brother pitted against brother. Double cross and betrayal were the order of the day. Often there wasn't enough to eat. Some of the children went off with strangers who promised them a loaf of bread if they cooperated."

"And Paros was behind it all," Lukas said.

"He was the leader." Father Sotiris turned his head and spat into the fire. "He called himself a patriot, and many people believed him. Only later, when the children didn't return, they realized he'd manipulated them. Hence the curse, ostracism."

"Is Paros wanted by any law enforcement agency now?" Lukas asked, his eyes on Nadia's shocked face.

The monk looked straight at him, but somehow his eyes seemed empty, as if his soul had gone out of them. "That I can't tell you. It's been so many years."

He pushed back his chair, the wooden legs scraping on the stone floor. Gathering his robes around him he stood up. "It is time to bid you good night. Sleep well, my children."

Without another word he shuffled out of the room, leaving his cane next to the fireplace. The cat on Nadia's lap suddenly stretched, jumped to the floor and loped silently out of the room after the monk.

She looked over at Lukas, who was staring into the dying fire. Outside, rain pattered onto the dry earth, releasing a fragrance that drifted through the screened window that served as ventilation for the kitchen. "I guess we might as well go to bed, too."

Lukas nodded. "There doesn't seem to be much else to do."

He banked the fire, sliding a portable screen across the front of the fireplace. Not that there was anything to burn if a spark flew out; walls, hearth and floor were of stone. He laid the monk's cane on the table so that the man would find it when he got up in the morning.

"Come, Nadia, let's get some sleep. In the morning the fisherman will be back for us. I can't say I'll be sorry to leave this place."

Nadia couldn't have agreed more.

Their room was much as they'd left it. Bedding lay neatly folded at the foot of the striped mattresses.

"Where did that come from?" Nadia exclaimed.

"Our host, I presume." Lukas's voice held a note of irony. "Unless he has a familiar spirit helping him with the household chores."

Nadia uttered a strained laugh. "That's not so hard to believe in this place."

IN THE DEEPEST HOURS of the night she started awake, sitting up on the cot. Despite the bite in the air of the unheated room, sweat beaded across her forehead. Not far from her, Lukas slept in a dimly visible lump on the other cot. His breathing was quiet, even.

Her heart still pounded in her chest. Had she had a nightmare that had been fearful enough to wake her? If so, she couldn't recall it.

Rain still fell, a soft staccato on the metal roof overhead. Below the cliff, the sea growled sullenly, as if it too slept, but dreamed of tomorrow.

She lay down again, hunching her shoulders under the inadequate blanket, wishing she'd brought a heavier nightgown or had kept a sweater nearby. She was on the edge of sleep when she heard it.

A high-pitched wailing and crying seemed to come from a great distance. Children's voices. She could distinguish one word. *Mama. Mama.* Over and over, sounding piteously forlorn.

She sprang out of bed, ignoring the cold that rushed up her legs as soon as her bare feet touched the stone floor. "Lukas." She leaped across the space separating them, and shook his shoulder. "Lukas, wake up."

The crying stopped for a moment, then began again.

"What?" Lukas struggled to sit up, the cot groaning.

"Lukas, do you hear it? The children crying."

She felt rather than saw him rub his eyes. "I told you, Nadia, there are no children here."

"I heard them," she insisted. "Listen."

He remained still, listening. A chilling fear ran icy fingers up his spine. He heard it. *Mama. Mama.*

Reason told him it was impossible. There were no children. There were no ghosts. But his ears told him otherwise. "It's only the wind." He groped to find his sneakers and his flashlight. "This place has more holes than a sieve."

As they stepped into the corridor, the sound of crying was all around them. Lukas snapped on the flashlight, sending a beam playing over walls. The light barely penetrated the darkness that clung to them like a damp fog.

The crying stopped abruptly.

There was not another sound, except the sighing of the wind through a hole in the roof of the corridor, and the slow drip of rain.

They went back to their beds, but Nadia couldn't sleep. Each time she closed her eyes, she saw the faces of the lost children and heard their cries, even though now they echoed only in her head. She was cold, her feet like icy stones; she couldn't get warm.

Then Lukas was beside her, crawling in next to her, ignoring the tortured creaks of the springs as he arranged his own blanket over them.

His body was as warm as a furnace. "Better?" he whispered, wrapping his arms around her waist. "You're shaking. And you're frozen."

"I couldn't seem to get warm." Her voice cracked on a near sob. "I kept hearing the children."

"There are no children," he repeated, almost as if he wanted to convince himself. "It was just the wind."

"I'm scared, Lukas. I don't like this place."

"Just between you and me, I'm scared, too. If there is such a thing as ghosts, this is where they live."

Nadia felt soothed by his words and warmed by his presence. Before long she fell asleep. If the warmth didn't reach the center of her it didn't matter.

She dreamed Lukas made love to her, his mouth hot on her breasts, his hands gentle as they moved over her body. She wasn't cold anymore.

When she awoke she was alone. Lukas, fully dressed, was folding blankets on the other cot. She hurried to get up, avoiding his eyes. Although he cast her an odd look, she said nothing.

IN THE KITCHEN the monk was already up, hunched over a book at the table, a book that Nadia saw had ornate illuminated headings on the fragile parchment pages. He looked up at their entry, a soft smile on his wrinkled face. "There is bread and milk for your breakfast," he said, indicating a round tin on the sideboard and a battered pot bubbling on the stove. "Eat before you go."

The milk tasted unlike any Nadia had ever drunk. "It's goat milk," Lukas explained. "Good for you."

She managed to choke down some of the hard bread by dipping it into the hot, sweetened milk. Thinking of the hike across the island, she forced herself to eat, although the events of the night had dampened her appetite.

Father Sotiris was still reading when they were ready to leave. Lukas extended a couple of thousand-drachma notes to him, but the old man shook his head. "I have no need for money," he said in his stilted French. "I have my home, my food and my cat. I need nothing else."

"Use it to repair the roof, buy something in the village," Lukas suggested.

"Barba Costas, the shepherd, brings me what I need. Go in peace."

Chapter Eight

A high wind combed the shrub-covered slopes of the island as they climbed the ridge on their way back to the boat dock. Overhead, the sky was a radiant blue. Two or three fluffy white clouds only served to emphasize its perfection. The sea murmured benignly today, an expanse of pure sapphire accented with little whitecaps that glistened like crystal.

Nadia inhaled the scent of rain-freshened leaves, and banished the cobwebs remaining from her disturbed night. "It feels as if it was all a bad dream."

"Perhaps it was." Lukas smiled whimsically.

As if their words had expressed skepticism for the course of events, the bell clanged behind them, confirming the reality of the monastery and its ghostly secrets.

"It wasn't always a monastery, you know," Lukas said soberly. "You may have noticed that the bell tower is much newer than the building."

Nadia suppressed a shudder as the bell tolled again, reverberating dissonantly over the hills. "So what was it?"

"It was a prison where they kept political dissenters, and the children before they transported them out of the country."

Nadia stumbled but managed to recover. Feeling as if her blood had turned to ice, she fought the faintness. The crying in the night—her imagination?

Her distress must have communicated itself to Lukas. He stopped, turning to face her. "Nadia, are you all right?"

She shook her head. "No, I'm not. Could any one be all right, knowing how people must have suffered?"

"It happened a long time ago." He cupped a hand gently around her cheek, stroking his thumb across her lips. "The best we can do is try to keep it from happening again."

They trudged on, passing the deserted corral where the sheep had been penned yesterday. There was no sign of the shepherd or his dog.

Instead of the morning commerce that should have brought people out into the streets, the village was empty and forlorn, as if all the residents had fled. A shutter banged in the wind. Dead leaves and dust blew along the gutters. Nothing else moved.

Nadia felt a momentary fear when she saw the deserted dock. Would the fisherman come to pick them up, or were they destined to spend the rest of their lives trapped on this island, like Odysseus?

As if he sensed her thoughts, Lukas squeezed her arm reassuringly. "Don't worry. He'll be here." He scanned the horizon, squinting against the brilliance of the sun reflected on the water. "See, there he comes now."

As the black speck far out to sea grew larger, the put-put of the caïque's engine drifted to them, carried on the wind.

Nadia had her pills with her, but in her relief at getting off the island, she doubted she'd need the medication. She sat comfortably in the back of the boat, not noticing the smell of diesel fuel and stale fish. But when Lukas sat down beside her and threw an arm around her shoulders, she pulled away.

He stared at her in surprise. "What's eating you? You were glad enough last night to have me near you."

Her dream of him had haunted her throughout their breakfast and their hike, not entirely erased by the eerie atmosphere of the island. "That was last night. This is now. This whole trip hasn't been productive enough. I'm worried about more time passing...."

He withdrew his arm, reflecting on the perversity of women in general, and this one in particular. Last night after she had fallen asleep, she had snuggled trustingly against him, as if they'd been sharing a bed for years. So closely that he'd become aroused; if they had been in any other place, under any other circumstances, he would have made love to her. As it was, he'd gotten up and returned to his own cot before she woke up and noticed his condition.

She was right, of course. Gerry's murder was the reason they were together at all. But at the moment, with the sun striking diamond sparks off the sea, the gentle surging of the boat under them and the firm but feminine weight of her body against him, danger seemed far away. Even though his better judgment told him he was taking a tremendous risk, he wanted to touch her.

And he couldn't quite convince himself she didn't want it, too. "We're safe here," he said. "You don't feel ill, do you?"

She considered, involuntarily pressing her hand against her midriff. "No, I'm fine. Do you think Halias will be waiting for us when we reach Igoumenitsa? Come to think of it, why do you suppose he didn't follow us to the island?"

One corner of Lukas's mouth turned down. "Probably because he knew something we didn't. That there was nothing to find on the island. So you can bet we'll be seeing him again."

"And what will you do?"

"Wait and see what he does first."

They were silent for a moment, listening to the beat of the engine and the soft rush of the water behind the boat. Nadia wriggled down into the cushions, stretching her long legs, clad today in faded jeans, in front of her. Why had she pushed Lukas away? Was she attempting to deny the dream she'd had in the night? She turned to regard his dark handsome profile. He had one knee drawn up and his arms wrapped around it for balance. His topaz eyes, framed by dense black lashes, were fixed on the horizon where the pale, box-shaped buildings of Igoumenitsa were taking form.

"Who's Dorian?"

His words, uttered in a quiet tone, made her jump. A warning system she didn't know she had sprang to life inside her. "Where did you hear that name?" she hedged, her mouth dry.

"People who share bedrooms should be careful what they say in their sleep."

"I didn't ask to share it," she retorted in a feeble effort to distract him. "It was the only room there was."

"So who's Dorian?" He didn't even bother to look at her.

Nadia sighed. What was the use? He'd keep on until he wormed it out of her. And in any case, what difference did it make?

"I was engaged to him for a year."

Lukas turned his head and his eyes seemed to glow hotter than the late-morning sun over their heads. "And?" He looked at her fingers. "I don't see a ring."

"Was," she said. "Past tense. We broke up more than two years ago."

Lukas's brows rose. "And you still dream about him?"

No, I dream about you. She clapped one hand over her mouth, afraid she'd say the words aloud. But his expression remained bland, questioning. "I don't remember."

"You must have been dreaming about something. You said, 'No, not like Dorian' and then just 'No.' You seemed upset. What happened between you?"

"It has nothing to do with you."

"Academic interest, shall we say? I want to know more about you. Is that a crime?"

"We're investigating a crime, in case you've forgotten. You don't need to know more about me."

"No," Lukas agreed. "But I'd like to."

"Why?"

But he didn't answer as the fisherman nudged the boat into the slip at the busy Igoumenitsa dock.

Lukas led her off the dock, then leaned over to pay the fisherman the agreed-upon fee. When they reached his car, Lukas walked around it carefully, inspecting the underside, the exhaust pipe, the trunk with an inordinate amount of care. Nothing appeared to have been disturbed.

Had Halias, guessing their destination, not followed them from Ioannina? That certainly appeared to be the case.

"Are you looking for a bomb?" Nadia asked, unable to suppress a shudder.

Lukas gave her a steady look. "It would be stupid to discount the possibility." He unlocked the car, after checking a small strip of transparent tape he'd stuck to the bottom of each door. "However, I think we're safe. For the moment."

"For the moment," Nadia repeated.

He reached across the seat to unlock the passenger door. "Do you want to leave now, before we get to Pefkaki and land in who knows what kind of hornet's nest?"

Nadia lifted her chin. "No. Whatever we find, I want to be there."

He had seen her shudder as she realized why he'd checked the car so minutely. She was scared all right, but she wasn't going to let the fear stop her. A woman with courage. He liked that.

In fact, he more than liked it. He started the car, listening to the engine turn over before engaging the gears and backing out of the parking space.

For an instant he regretted not following through on the desire he'd felt in the night, even as he reminded himself that deeper involvement with her would seriously impede their search.

Yet on a purely masculine level, it irked him that she seemed oblivious to the attraction he'd sensed since the morning after her arrival in Athens.

"Is Dorian the one who set you against men?" he asked, throwing out a deliberate challenge.

Out of the corner of his eye, he saw a muscle tense in her jaw. "I have nothing against men."

"But you've decided you don't need them."

"I was glad you were there last night," she admitted, although she wasn't quite sure why. Probably it was the oddly unsettled feeling she'd carried from the island, combined with gratitude to him for not sending her summarily back to Athens after Halias appeared. She felt she owed him something.

He looked comically startled by her honesty. "Ah!"

A reluctant smile tugged at the corner of Nadia's mouth. "What's that supposed to mean? You did what any friend would have done."

"Friend?" His hands tightened on the steering wheel.

Before long, they arrived in Ioannina. Lukas stopped the car in front of the hotel where they'd spent the night, having arranged with the manager to take messages for them there.

Nadia waited in the car, but as the sun rose straight overhead at noon, she grew thirsty. She got out and walked into the hotel, blinking as her eyes grew accustomed to the dimness.

Lukas stood by the kiosk that sold magazines and sundries at the side of the lobby. One foot braced on the rung of a chair as he held the telephone receiver to his ear. The conversation was in Greek. Nadia couldn't pick out a word, not even references to Paros or Halias.

What was he talking about? And to whom?

She took an iced bottle of orange drink from the cooler, paying the man in the kiosk. Lukas put up one finger, indicating he was almost finished.

When he hung up the phone and had counted out the coins to pay the long-distance toll, he came over to her, taking the bottle from her hand and drinking a long swallow.

"Any news?" she asked.

"Not much." He handed back the bottle and she drank the remainder of the tart-sweet liquid, imagining she tasted Lukas's flavor on the rounded mouth of the bottle. "Gabriel says Halias is a mercenary, apparently a free-lancer who hires out to whoever can pay him."

"So he was trying to kill us." Too much had happened for Nadia to be shocked by the bald statement.

"Not necessarily. If he was, he would have succeeded. Someone's trying to scare us off."

Nadia smiled grimly, her facial muscles tightening. "But we're not going to let them, are we?"

Lukas looked at her with undisguised respect. "No, we're not."

She linked her arm into his. "Then let's get started. To Pefkaki."

"Okay." He patted her hand where it lay in the crook of his elbow. "But let's pick up some fruit and bread to eat on the way. No telling what we'll find up there."

As if their conversation in the hotel had defused some of the tension between them, they were able to chat easily as they drove north from Ioannina. They finished the bread and fruit when Lukas turned off the paved highway to follow a narrow road that deteriorated into a track of ruts and rocks.

Before long, they paused in front of a makeshift army bridge that stretched across a swiftly rushing stream at the bottom of a deep gorge, replacing the span that had been washed out.

"Do you think it's safe?" Nadia bit her lip, staring at the foaming rapids that thundered below.

"Safe enough," Lukas assured her. "They always test it with an army truck. Jolie is about a quarter the weight of one of those."

They negotiated the roughened planks, which creaked loudly in protest. The structure swayed under the car but held. Nadia didn't let out her pent-up breath until the four wheels rested securely on solid ground once more. The road grew narrower, little more than a shelf that clung to the edge of the mountain before them. They crossed a ridge, then before them, in a little valley verdant with newly green trees, a church dome caught the last light of the sun as it fell behind a mountain to the west.

Night came early here. The village lay in shadow by the time they reached the main square, although the sky remained a limpid turquoise overhead.

The square was deserted in the dying light, with shops shuttered and their doors locked. The buildings were of gray stone although pots of geraniums provided little patches of color that relieved the monotony. Rough cobblestones paved the streets.

Getting out of the car, Nadia shivered, assailed by the same eerie dread that had afflicted her on the island. "Where is everyone?"

Before Lukas could venture an opinion, the church bell tolled, a booming sound that echoed through the deep valley. A pair of black-clad women wearing white kerchiefs over their heads appeared from behind the closed butcher shop. Their eyes fixed straight ahead, they walked across the square and disappeared through the open door of the church.

Following the women, an old man with a cane stumped into the church, then a family group including two girls in royal-blue school uniforms.

"At least there are children here," Lukas muttered.

More people appeared and were swallowed up by the dark cavern of the church. Some of them passed within a few feet of Nadia and Lukas standing next to the Renault, seemingly oblivious to the newcomers' presence. The people were intent only on answering the summons of the tolling bell.

When they had all gone inside, the bell stopped clanging. The voice of the priest drifted faintly over the square. Even Nadia, not understanding the words, perceived the deep sadness in the rising and falling cadence of the chant.

"Holy Thursday," Lukas said quietly. "It's almost as important as Good Friday." He reached into the car for her suitcase and his pack. "Come on, Nadia. There's supposed to be a hotel in this place."

The small village's hotel had a couple of rooms above a coffee shop. A heavyset man with grizzled hair and small piglike eyes set in a deep network of wrinkles wiped the bar separating the tables from the kitchen area. None of the tables was occupied. It appeared that everyone was at the church.

After they entered, the man reached under the bar and flicked a hidden switch. A single bulb hanging on a cord in the center of the room began to glow, but so feebly that it did little to augment the lamp over the bar.

"We'd like two rooms, please," Lukas said in a tone that said he wasn't going to take excuses.

The man's expression didn't change. "I have two rooms, but one is paid to the end of the month."

"By whom?" Lukas asked, although he could make a guess.

The man pulled out a worn box and riffled through the index cards. "Gerald Parker."

"That's my brother," Nadia exclaimed, understanding the name despite the odd pronunciation. "He stayed here?"

"So it would seem," Lukas said. "Not too surprising. What surprises me—" He broke off, switching to Greek as he addressed the man once more.

"Gerald Parker is dead. Why are you keeping his room?"

Something flickered through the man's small eyes. It might have been fear. "Yes, yes, he's dead. But he paid through this week, and his things are still in the room."

His things. Lukas clenched his fist as he repressed a surge of rage at the incompetence of the village police. They were supposed to confiscate the dead man's belongings and turn them over to Lukas when he arrived. Although he hadn't yet met with the local constable, he'd expected more efficiency. Now he was faced with the problem of having to inspect them in front of Nadia. Seeing Gerry's things would be a shock for her, one he would rather lead up to gently. He wouldn't say anything to her just yet.

"Give us the other room," he said. "I trust it has two beds."

The man nodded. "Your identification, please."

Standard procedure, yet it gave Lukas an uncomfortable sensation to hand over his ID, the card that destroyed any chance he'd have to appear ordinary. Villagers liked to keep to themselves, and they might close ranks against what they perceived as outside interference. Now he couldn't probe as much as he needed to. *What the hell,* at least he could probe through Gerry's belongings. He would do that as soon as Nadia was asleep.

"I'd like to see where they buried him," Nadia said as they climbed the wooden staircase with its creaking treads. "Could we go now, before it gets completely dark?"

"Okay, just let me put the luggage away." She didn't know yet that they were to share a room again. Time enough later to deal with that.

THE NEATLY FENCED CEMETERY bordered by cypress trees that thrust their points into a darkening sky, was a short walk outside the village. The deep green needles lent an astringent perfume to the mauve twilight.

Last summer's grass crackled under their feet as Lukas and Nadia walked between the rows of simple tombstones, interspersed with an occasional ornate marble cross. The charnel house was a low silhouette at the far side of the plot.

"Here it is," Nadia said softly. Even in Greek, the upper case letters were recognizable. Nothing else distinguished the grave from any other in the cemetery. There were no fresh flowers, no lighted candle.

Nadia stood looking down at the plain granite stone, the freshly carved letters not yet weathered like those on the others around her.

Why?

Her parents had tried to teach her acceptance, but deep down anger surged. Such a wasted life. Gerald didn't deserve this, a lonely grave on a remote mountain.

"Nadia."

She had almost forgotten Lukas's presence, and looked around, her eyes burning with tears that refused to fall.

"Nadia," he said gently, "it's all right to cry."

"Oh, Lukas, I'm too angry to cry. I want to get the person who did this."

She took a step toward him and stumbled on a hillock of tough, dry grass. He caught her, folding her against his body. The dam burst at his touch. Like a child she buried her face in the front of his shirt, sobbing out her sorrow and rage, until she could cry no more. She mopped up with a handkerchief he gave her.

The outburst left her drained, barely able to keep her feet as they groped their way out of the cemetery and found the path leading back to the village. She kept her head down, picking her way over the packed earth and rocks.

It was almost fully dark. Thorn bushes clawed at their clothes whenever they strayed from the path. A faint breeze carried the chanting of the priest toward them, indicating the mass was not yet over. For the moment an aura of peace hung over the valley.

But it was short-lived. Suddenly a sharp crack reverberated from the surrounding cliffs.

As Nadia jerked up her head, her eyes widening in horror, Lukas swayed and crumpled at her feet.

Chapter Nine

A second shot rang out. Nadia threw herself down next to Lukas as she distinctly felt the whoosh of air next to her head, as if a fast-flying insect had skimmed her cheek. Fear tasted harsh and metallic in her mouth. She swallowed hard, fighting nausea. The suffocating smell of dust filled her nostrils, her throat, choking her.

"Lukas," she cried hoarsely.

He lay facedown on the rocky path, not moving. Lifting herself cautiously, making sure her head would not poke above the shrubs that surrounded them, she crept up beside him.

He was heavy, almost too heavy for her to turn over. Crouched on her knees, panting with exertion, she managed to get him onto his back. He groaned, his lips moving. The sound sent a rush of relief through her as she examined him.

He wasn't dead. He wasn't dead.

Night shrouded the valley, but there was enough residual light for her to see the angry mark about his temple and the blood that matted his hairline. A dark rivulet trickled sluggishly down his cheek.

"Lukas, can you hear me?"

She ran her hands over his body, searching for wounds.

"Ouch."

Nadia nearly jumped out of her skin, her fingers clenching on the hard muscle of his leg. "Lukas, are you all right?"

"If you keep doing that, I will be." His voice was only just above a whisper, with labored spaces between the words, as if he could hardly breathe.

"Doing what?" Nadia gulped in several deep breaths, hyperventilating in her relief.

"Rubbing my thigh like that. Gently, though. I think I've got a few bruises."

She snatched her hand away. "Does your head hurt? I think you've been shot."

He lifted his hand, the movement slow since his arm suddenly seemed to weigh a ton. Delicately he probed the wound, swearing under his breath as the numbness faded and a throbbing pain began. He lowered his hand and braced it against the rough ground, trying to push himself up. With a groan, he fell back heavily, cursing anew.

"Lukas, I don't think you should move. You've probably got a concussion." Nadia kept her hands fixed on his shoulders to keep him in place. "You need a doctor."

The sound he made resembled a laugh. "I doubt if there's a doctor here. Besides, I never really passed out. I was only stunned. I couldn't move for a moment."

"Well, it's obvious that you can't move now, either," she said angrily. "And we can't stay here all night. I'll have to get help."

He grasped her wrist and tugged, showing surprising strength. "Nadia, wait. It could be dangerous. We can't trust anyone in the village. And whoever shot us is still waiting—"

"I'll be careful." She bit her lip, her mind racing to form a plan. Could she get the car up here? She tried to remember the configuration of the cobbled streets. Beside her, Lukas's breathing was labored as he fought against the pain and the weakness. "If I bring the car to the end of the path, can you make it down there?"

"After I rest a little, probably." His voice took on a desperate urgency. "But Nadia, he could be waiting. He could try again."

"But it's dark now," she argued. "I'll stay in the shadows."

"It was almost dark before. He's probably using a night scope. Darkness is no hindrance to his aim, if that's the case."

"I'll be careful." She shivered as a cold gust of wind cut through her sweater. The chanting of the priest not far away reached a crescendo, only serving to underscore their isolation. No one in the village had heard the shot; they were all in the church. No one was coming to their aid. "It's going to be cold tonight. We can't stay here."

Lukas knew she was right. He closed his eyes, partly to block out the pain, partly to stifle his compulsion to protect her. It infuriated him that he was helpless but there was nothing to do but allow Nadia to get the car. "Okay." He pressed her wrist, barely noticing the little whimper she made. "Just watch it. And trust no one." He groped under his sweater. "Here, take my gun."

She stared at it, the gray metal gleaming faintly in the starlight. She shook her head. "No, I can't. I don't know anything about guns. I'd probably shoot my foot off. Besides, what if this killer comes after you? You need the gun. I'll keep out of sight."

Reluctantly he conceded she was right. He let his gun-holding hand fall across his chest. "See that you do."

He listened to the snapping of twigs as she scrambled down the hill. His head pounded in a vicious echo of his own heartbeat. He tried to separate his thoughts from the pain, setting each into compartments. He'd been shot before, once much more severely than this; he knew something about bullet wounds.

In any case, this wasn't a bullet wound. If it had been, he'd be dead. What had hit him was a rock chip from a bullet ricocheting from a crag that loomed over the path. It had grazed the bone along his eye socket, barely missing the soft temple.

Leaving the gun lying on his chest, he touched the wound. The bleeding had already stopped, but the grittiness under his fingers told him the wound needed a thorough cleansing. He was sure he didn't have a concussion because he'd never been completely unconscious at any time.

He cursed fluently to himself, startling a bird that shrieked as it flew out of the thorn bushes. The shooting only bore out his fears. He had left Nadia exposed as he lay dazed, unable to move. No thanks to him, the second shot had missed her and she'd had the sense to get down. He'd never have been able to forgive himself if she'd been shot.

And he'd had to let her go, perhaps into greater danger. Clenching his teeth, he hoisted himself up to a sitting position, then to his feet. He swayed, fighting the waves of giddiness that came over him. His head was a solid mass of agony, and he bit the inside of his cheek, drawing blood as he focused his mind on the next to impossible task of placing one foot before the other.

NADIA CREPT down the path, bent nearly double to keep her head low. Every time a pebble shot out from under her foot or a twig snapped, she tensed, listening for the chilling crack of another shot.

With an odd clarity of perception she thought about the fact that a shot might well be the last sound she heard on earth. Would the entry of the bullet hurt?

Very likely. She had seen Lukas's agony, despite his efforts to hide it from her. But perhaps if the shot were fatal, she would die before she registered the pain.

Morbid, she told herself. *Get your act together.*

At the end of the path stretched a cobblestone street only fit for mules, but she was sure she could maneuver the car up it. The rhythmic chanting in the church seemed to envelop her as she sneaked around the buildings, keeping to the deepest shadows. Streetlights were few and far between, making it easier.

At the edge of the square she stopped. Jolie stood at one side but standard lamps illuminated the area here too brightly. If she walked across the square she would present a perfect target to the rifleman.

The ring of car keys dug into her palm as she balled her fist. She clutched the door key between her first and second finger, while the ignition key protruded between her last two fingers. She mustn't get them mixed up. Timing could mean everything.

She circled the square, keeping clear of the pools of light. The little Renault stood in such a way that the passenger side was in dense shadow. If she could get in from that side and slide over into the driver's seat—

Crouching as low as possible, she made a run for it, skidding to a stop next to the door. Nothing happened. No sound, except the melancholy singing: *Kýrie èléison,* Lord, have mercy. During a lull, a dog barked far up the mountainside.

Edging close until her eyes were level with the window molding, she peered into the car. Since it had no back seat, there wasn't much space for anyone to hide. The lamp cast a swathe of light across both bucket seats. Empty.

Reassured, she inserted the key into the lock. *Damn,* she couldn't turn it. She wriggled the key, hoping to unjam the lock. Perspiration broke out on her skin and trickled down between her breasts.

After a moment, the lock gave. She realized she hadn't pushed the key in far enough at first. Crawling in until she lay across the two seats, she pushed the ignition key into place and scrambled into the driver's seat, closing the door behind her. The faint click of the latch sounded louder to her ears than the earlier rifle shot.

Cautiously sitting up, she surveyed the area once more, knowing the headrest on the back of the seat would make her invisible from behind.

Praying the car would start on the first try, she floored the clutch and turned the key, while also depressing the gas pedal lightly. *Thank God,* Gerald had taught her how to drive a standard shift car. Without those lessons and her subsequent years with a recalcitrant MG, she would have been helpless.

The car started with a roar that made her jump. She released her foot, which was allowing too much gas to reach the carburetor, and shifted into first gear. The engine sound must have carried to the people in the church, for at that moment a woman, her white scarf almost a beacon in the darkness, peered around the open doorway.

In her haste, Nadia let out the clutch too quickly. The little car leaped forward as if on fire, and Nadia had to jerk the steering wheel around to avoid colliding with a lamppost. Then she was in the street, speeding over the cobbles but with the car firmly under control.

She had done it. Now to reach Lukas.

But her momentary elation turned to stark terror. A man was standing in the middle of the street; his feet braced in an arrogant stance as he cradled the rifle in his arms with deceptive negligence. Nadia knew it was deceptive, because when she didn't slow the car he lifted it casually to his shoulder and aimed it at her.

She saw the scope mounted on the barrel, confirming Lukas's guess. The distance was such that the man couldn't possibly miss. In the narrow street, walled in by stone buildings, she had no place to swerve.

She would die, and so might Lukas in the chilly night if she didn't reach him.

A cold fatalism gripped her, driving out terror. Her mouth so dry she couldn't swallow, she slowed fractionally, assessing the space between the waiting killer and the stone wall of a warehouse.

As she approached, she could make out the icy features of Halias.

He waited calmly, as if time meant nothing to him now that he had her in his sights. Why didn't he shoot? her mind screamed. *Get it over!*

Summoning all her willpower she gunned the engine, flooring the accelerator. Even she was astonished at the sudden burst of speed that shoved her back against the seat as if she'd been struck by a battering ram. A heavy thud reverberated sickeningly and she realized Halias had been hit. The rifle flew into her line of vision and clattered across the hood.

She didn't dare think of what had happened to the man as she battled with the car.

Jolie teetered on two wheels, then righted herself as the tires found traction on the uneven cobbles. Nadia sent her vehicle speeding out of the street and into the rutted road beyond. A glance in the rearview mirror showed Halias rising stiffly to his feet, shaking his fist at her. The rifle lay on the ground. She hoped she had smashed it to smithereens.

To her surprise Lukas was waiting at the bottom of the path resting in a seated position against the gnarled trunk of an undernourished pine.

He seemed more alert, able to get to his feet and make his way to the car with minimal help from her. "Any trouble?" he asked, welcoming her support as they rounded the back of the car.

"Not with the car," she said. "I made out our friend Halias as the one who was doing the shooting. He tried to stop me in the street back there, but I knocked him over with the car."

"With the car?" Lukas echoed. "Did you do any damage?" He sounded faint, and his weight strained her aching shoulders.

"We've almost been killed and you're thinking of your car?" she burst out incredulously, fear suddenly hitting her and making her knees buckle. She stiffened her muscles but the trembling increased until she would have fallen, had she and Lukas not been holding each other up.

"Not the car, idiot," he snarled. "That fool Halias. I hope you made it a direct hit."

She shook her head, pinching full lips together. "No. It was only a glancing blow. He was shaking his fist at me when I last saw him."

"Damn."

The struggle to get into the car seemed to drain him. Lukas fell silent as Nadia drove back to the hotel, the street on which she had encountered Halias now empty. The church, too, was dark and deserted. Sometime during the confusion the mass must have ended, with no one aware of the deadly drama that had been enacted outside.

At their inn's coffee shop, several tables were occupied. Nadia sagged with relief at the sight of the old men clicking worry beads between gnarled fingers. She had been wondering, in view of everything that had happened, if the people they'd seen earlier would have vanished into thin air.

Lukas had tied his handkerchief like a runner's headband around his forehead to hide the wound. Since they had no water to wipe the blood from his cheek, he was careful to keep that side of his face turned away from their landlord as he requested the key. They must still have made an odd spectacle, covered with dust and bits of twigs as they toiled up the stairs, but the man said nothing.

"One room?" Nadia exclaimed as Lukas closed the door before leaning wearily against it.

"That's all they have." He struggled to speak as the lighted room dimmed before his eyes. Nadia seemed to waver, as if she stood at a distance and under water. "The other room is taken." He felt his knees about to give way. "Nadia, please—"

It was then she saw how ashen his skin had become. Quickly she reached over and slung his arm across her shoulder just as his legs buckled. They staggered to the bed. He was almost a dead weight, and fell so heavily that when she lost her grip on him the springs twanged.

He lay panting to catch his breath, his eyes squeezed shut in pain. He was only peripherally aware that Nadia was taking off his shoes. The floorboards creaked as she walked to the washstand. He heard the water slosh from the pitcher into the basin.

When he felt the cool caress of a wet towel on his face, he forced his heavy eyelids up. "Nadia, there's a first aid kit in my pack. It's got a bottle of disinfectant and bandages."

"First I'll wash the dirt out." She untied the handkerchief. The wound, she saw, was a shallow groove, but not as bad as the earlier bleeding had indicated.

Gently she wiped it with the wet cloth, working out all the bits of dirt and gravel. It began to bleed again, but only slightly. *Good,* she thought; the fresh blood would further cleanse the wound.

The disinfectant stung. Lukas let out an involuntary moan as the soaked cotton wool touched him. Nadia clenched her teeth in sympathy but kept doggedly cleaning the wound. With gauze and tape she formed a neat bandage that could be covered by his hair, if he didn't comb it too neatly.

"There, I think you'll live. Good thing you've got a hard skull." She went to the washstand and poured fresh water into a glass, bringing it back to him along with a couple of painkillers from a bottle in the first aid kit. "And these should take care of some of the headache."

"Yes, nurse." He swallowed the tablets obediently, his grateful smile hidden by the glass as he drank the water. "Now, how about if you get us something to eat?"

She blinked at him. "You want to eat?"

"Sure. Don't you?"

"What about Halias?"

Lukas shrugged, wincing at the movement. Fortunately the painkillers were already taking effect, the clawing agony now nothing more than a dull ache. "After his adventure with you and the car, he'll probably leave us alone for the night. Besides, I doubt if he'd want witnesses to his dirty work."

She nodded. "And where do I get us something to eat?"

"The man downstairs could probably fix something. It'll be vegetarian though since it's Holy Week."

Nadia's stomach growled, and she suddenly realized how hungry she was. "Long as it's filling, I don't care." She started for the door, then paused. "How do I communicate? I don't suppose he knows any French the way the monk did."

"Not likely." Lukas elbowed himself up higher in the bed, feeling better with every passing minute. "Give me a piece of paper and I'll write a note."

It struck Nadia as Lukas laboriously scribbled on the paper how much she depended on him. She must have been crazy to have considered investigating Gerald's death on her own, with or without the consent of Greek authorities. The language barrier alone, never mind her abysmal ignorance of the culture here, would have been insurmountable. The old monk had spoken French, but she hadn't heard an English word uttered since leaving Athens, except from Lukas and the hard-faced assassin Halias.

Lukas finished the note and handed it to her along with some drachma.

In the coffee shop only one table was occupied. Their landlord sat talking with two men who wore the black woolen cloaks of shepherds slung over their shoulders. Three pairs of dark, fathomless eyes stared at Nadia as she came down the stairs. The three men got up at once, the scrape of their chairs on the bare floor grating on her ears. With soft-spoken *Kaliníchtas*, the shepherds went out into the night.

Nadia handed the coffee shop owner the note and the money. He read it in silence, pocketing the money. Still without a word or a change of expression, he prepared a tray of steaming soup and chunks of bread.

"*Efharisto,*" she stammered, hesitantly trying her one Greek word. "Thank you."

The man nodded.

Upstairs, she found Lukas sprawled on the bed under the covers. His clothes lay in a dusty heap on the floor.

He was sound asleep.

Setting the tray on the table that stood between the beds, Nadia stared at him. He breathed easily, his lips slightly parted when he exhaled. His color had returned. Kneeling beside the bed, she lightly touched his temple, pleased to note that the skin around the bandage felt cool under her fingers and was not swollen or red. By tomorrow he would be himself again.

She hadn't meant to wake him, but suddenly realized his breathing had altered. Before she could get up from the floor, his hand snaked out to grasp her wrist. With a strength she wouldn't have thought him capable of under the influence of painkillers, he pulled her up on the bed, on top of him.

"Lukas! What are you doing?"

"Nadia." His eyes were closed, his voice slurred. Was he asleep or awake? Maybe he had a concussion after all and was hallucinating.

But the pressure his hand bore as he buried it in her hair, and the heat that burned through the bed covers from his body into hers, felt more like miraculously restored health.

She struggled, although she wasn't sure why. His embrace felt right and reminded her of last night, when she had needed his comfort to drive away the threatening darkness. "Lukas, let go. I've brought us some food."

"Mmm." His grip tightened.

She braced a hand against his shoulder to push herself up, but it slipped. Losing her balance, she landed in an even more ignominious sprawl next to him on the narrow bed, her face tucked against his neck.

His distinctive aroma filled her senses. Healthy male sweat and a trace of sandalwood from his after-shave. Memories of the times he'd come close to her mingled with the dream she'd had last night, the dream that was becoming more real every moment.

He cared about her. She knew he did. He wasn't like Dorian who'd always put his own interests ahead of hers. Independent woman though she was, she couldn't even resent Lukas's attempts to talk her into returning to Athens. She realized he wanted to protect her, shelter her from harm.

She turned her head to look at him. Black stubble covered his jaws, softening the hard angles. He hadn't shaved since yesterday morning, but she decided she liked the faintly scruffy look this gave him.

He smiled slightly, as if he felt her scrutiny despite his closed eyes. As all thought of escaping from his arms vanished, she couldn't stop her own smile.

Lifting her hand, she brushed back the unruly curls that fell onto his forehead. Her fingers encountered the bandage. She froze. Her heart thudded.

She could have lost him. Like she'd lost Gerry.

"Lukas, hold me." She no longer cared about pride, or the danger of giving part of herself to a man who could never belong to her. She wanted only to bask in his warmth, feel his arms locked around her, to forget all but the magic of this moment.

Chapter Ten

"Nadia."

His breath was sweet as it drifted over her face, his mouth warm as it came down to cover hers. He probed lightly and Nadia had no thought of evasion or escape. She closed her eyes against the glare of the overhead light bulb. The astringent scent of fresh sweat and the musk of warm skin swam in her head.

The sheet and several thick woolen blankets separated them, but even then she could feel the hardness of his body. She had only a moment to register her amazement that the wound and the painkillers had done nothing to impair his desire or his ability to realize it. Conscious thought faded as she submerged herself in a symphony of sensations.

THE MOON HAD moved out of range of the window before they stirred from their delicious lassitude. Smiling at each other, but unwilling to let words destroy the dream they had shared, they got up to eat. Wrapped in blankets, they sat on the bed, eating the vegetable stew from the rough pottery bowls. Even cold, accompanied by the hard, dry bread, it tasted wonderful.

Afterward they wrapped their arms around each other and slept—in a bed that was far too narrow for two people—but not for two lovers.

NADIA WOKE SUDDENLY, startled out of a dream whose remnants were already floating out of reach of her conscious mind. The room was draped in darkness, but a glance at the illuminated dial of her watch told her it was near dawn. A wolf howled, a lonely keening that floated down the valley. She shuddered but Lukas slept on, his head pillowed on her breast. Under his neck, her arm was numb.

Gently she withdrew it, not wanting to wake him while she gathered her thoughts.

He uttered an odd little grunt and she felt his eyelashes flutter against her skin. "Nadia, what is it?"

Trepidation made her stall. "How are you feeling?"

He shook his head, reaching up and gingerly touching his bandage. "Okay, I guess. No headache, although I wouldn't want to run a marathon right now. Why did you wake me?"

"I didn't," she protested. "Well, maybe I did. Lukas, did Gerald rent this room or the one next to us?"

The sharp intake of his breath told her he hadn't expected this question. "The one next door."

Suspicions whirled through her mind. Why had Lukas told her the room was taken? Gerald certainly had no need of it. Unless—

She sat up abruptly, pulling the blankets around her shoulders as the cold air hit her bare skin. "Lukas, why didn't you tell me?" A new thought struck her. "Are Gerry's things still in the room? We never got them and thought they'd just been delayed."

The room was beginning to lighten, the rising sun coating the Spartan furnishings a dull gray. She could see Lukas's closed expression, the hooded eyes that were wary and guarded. "Yes, I think his things are still in the room. He paid to the end of the month, the man said. I thought it would upset you."

"Upset me?" Nadia echoed, giving way to anger. "Didn't you think I had a right to know?"

Lukas nodded, avoiding her stormy blue eyes. "Of course you had a right. I was going to tell you as soon as I'd had a chance to look at the room. After all, I'm the cop. The investigation takes precedence over personal feelings."

An icy chill enveloped her body. "Then I'm sorry I interfered by asking for your comfort. And I hope last night's, uh—" Her breath caught in what could have been a sob. With an effort she controlled the trembling of her lower lip. "I hope last night's interlude wasn't too arduous for you."

He flipped over onto his side, trapping her between his body and the rough stucco wall. His eyes were copper pools of rage as he grasped her shoulder, shaking her. "Arduous," he repeated. "Arduous? And are you calling what we did last night a mere interlude?"

"Well, wasn't it?" she challenged. She kept her eyes fixed on him, hoping her own anger would mask the deep hurt he'd inflicted. Last night had meant so much to her. His tenderness had touched the deeply vulnerable core of her soul, and she had known there would never be another man for her like Lukas. Now to find it had all been a sham—

"Damn it, Nadia, you know it wasn't that." He hesitated, searching for words, weighing the wisdom of blurting out his feelings. "You know it was so much more." He felt some of the stiffness go out of her body as he lifted a hand and smoothed back the heavy golden mane from her forehead, tucking the thick locks behind her ear. "Nadia, I think I'm falling in love with you."

The misunderstanding was over as quickly as it had started. She stared at him, suspended between disbelief and a dawning wonder. "In—love—with—me?" She swallowed hard. "Lukas, you're crazy. Why, you hardly know me."

"I've seen enough to know that you've got courage like few people I've known. You've got no bad habits that irritate me. You're delicious to be with, and that golden mane of yours would cause a sensation at an Athens club."

She pushed him so that he fell flat on his back. A grin spread over his face. After a moment she laughed, too.

Only for an instant. The idea was tempting, but impossible. She had her work in Vancouver. He had his life here. It was just impossible.

She gave him a playful poke in the ribs. "Come on, Stylianos—what a mouthful that is—get up. I want to have a look at Gerry's room. Maybe there's something there that'll help us."

THEY DRESSED QUICKLY, shivering in the cold room. Nadia opened the window to let in the fresh morning air. A low ground mist was rising up the sides of the mountains, soon to be burned away by the sun's rays. Out of sight around the corner, the church bell clanged dolefully, a single melancholy note repeated over and over again.

"Good Friday," Lukas said. "Probably the most portentous day on the Orthodox calendar."

Nadia looked at him, noting his solemnity. "It's important to you, isn't it?"

Lukas shrugged. "Yes. We may seem very casual about it, but tradition and faith are deeply ingrained in every Greek." He turned from the window, his thoughts going from the sublime to the mundane. "Do you want first turn in the bathroom?"

GERALD'S ROOM was smaller than theirs, with a single bed against one wall. The door hadn't even been locked. A table littered with paper, magazines and opened mail took up most of the remaining space. The corner of a suitcase protruded from under the bed. A chest drawer hung out half open, a shirt sleeve dangling over the edge.

Except for a coating of dust on every surface, the room looked as if its occupant had just stepped out and would be back momentarily.

Nadia was torn between anger and sorrow for Gerry's untimely death, just as she'd felt in the cemetery.

She shook her head. The village with its desolate air, the hypnotic tolling of the bell—all of it was making her crazy, destroying her perspective. But she couldn't tell Lukas what she thought.

"Why weren't his things packed and shipped home?" she asked suddenly, curiosity taking over. "It looks as if no one's been in this room since Gerry left for the last time. Wouldn't the police have wanted to search for clues to his death?"

Lukas was wondering the same thing himself. But he knew that since the case involved a foreigner, the local constable would expect the Athens police, in the person of Lukas, to deal with it. Knowing Lukas was on the way, he'd no doubt decided to postpone packing Gerald's belongings. It was the only explanation.

Nadia spoke again before Lukas could frame an answer that would satisfy her.

"Lukas, where are his wallet and his passport? He had them on him when he was—killed, didn't he?"

"Yes. I've got them. They were sent to Athens. I was going to give them to you as soon as this was over."

Nadia sifted through the papers on the table, noting the surveyors' charts, a couple of books on geology, and oddly, a copy of Ian Fleming's *The Man with the Golden Gun*. The writing paper was blank, as was a spiral-bound notepad. The only item that had the remotest bearing on their investigation was a detailed map of the surrounding mountains pinned to the wall. Footpaths and elevations were noted on it, and the location of the disputed marble quarry had been circled with a fluorescent yellow marker.

"I wonder—" Nadia stared at the map, her teeth biting into her lower lip.

Lukas came up behind her, resting one hand on her shoulder. "I wonder, too. Did he have some reason for coming up here other than his business with the quarry?"

Nadia picked up one of the geology books, leafing idly through it. As she was about to put it down, a photo dropped out and fluttered onto the desk.

"Hello, what's this?" Lukas held it up to the light. A faded image of a handsome man with white hair and compelling dark blue eyes stared back at him.

"Let me see that." Lukas handed it over. "This must be Andreas Paros." Her heart pounded in excitement. "The resemblance to Gerald is remarkable. I wonder where he got it?"

"From your mother, perhaps?"

Nadia shook her head. "Not likely. I don't think Sally had any pictures of Andreas. She wanted to forget him, remember? And this looks to be of recent vintage. It's been more than thirty years since Sally left him." She looked at Lukas. "Do you want it?"

"Keep it for now. It may come in handy when we talk to people around the village. If Paros is here, we'll find him."

"What about the gunman Halias?"

"My guess is that he'll lie low, at least until night. If he's trying to kill us, he won't want any witnesses. One murder here is bad enough, if someone's got something to hide. Two more would bring down a crowd of police. Which reminds me, I should check in with my office."

One or two tables were occupied when they entered the coffee shop below. The men looked up, curiosity and an odd wariness in their eyes as they regarded the strangers who invaded their domain. The owner was in his usual place, polishing the bar. Lukas paused to exchange a few words with him, laying their room key on the polished marble.

"He speaks," Nadia said as they stepped out the door into the bright spring morning.

"Of course he speaks."

"He didn't say a word last night when I got our food," Nadia said indignantly.

Lukas laughed. "He's probably just shy. This isn't exactly the place to learn all the social amenities."

"Did you ask him about Gerald's room?"

"They knew I was coming here. He says the local constable told him to leave it until I arrived. I think it's time we had a talk with the gentleman."

"What about breakfast?"

He pretended astonishment. "You mean you're not planning to fast all day?"

"Fast?" she repeated. "Is that what everyone's doing?"

"Some do, some don't." Lukas laughed and took her hand in his, linking their fingers. "We'll get something to eat first."

Breakfast was a Spartan meal, taken in a taverna that subbed as the village *pâtisserie*. It consisted of bread and lavishly sugared milk, which they consumed under the disapproving stare of an elderly woman.

"What was her problem?" Nadia asked later as she inhaled the crisp mountain air. She and Lukas were hiking the rough steep trail that led to the edge of town where the police station was located. "She acted as if we were committing a mortal sin."

"To her we were," Lukas said bluntly. "It was the milk. Milk is forbidden on Good Friday except in certain circumstances, such as for children or in sickness."

"Oh," said Nadia. "But what else was there? We had to eat something."

Lukas patted her arm in an understanding manner. "It's okay, Nadia. I don't hold with all these rules myself."

A young man typed industriously at a machine Nadia had only seen at antique auctions as they entered the little building. Warnings about forest fires and emergency procedures in the event of earthquakes framed the outer doorway. The sturdy oak desk was almost invisible under mounds of paper and mail, obviously just delivered. Two coffee cups filled the only vacant corner. A single bulb suspended from the water-marked ceiling provided the only lighting.

The young man looked up at their entrance. *"Kal-iméra."* Good morning. Nadia understood that much.

"Good morning," Lukas answered courteously. "Is Constable Demos in?" He reached into his pocket and withdrew his police identification, which he showed the other. "You might tell him Lukas Stylianos is here about the Parker case."

The man looked flustered. "Kýrie Stylianos. I'm terribly sorry. If he'd known—" He cleared his throat. "Constable Demos is up at the marble quarry. Some kind of labor dispute. He was called away earlier. We didn't know you were here. Or rather, we didn't know who you were—" The man's voice trailed off, his face turning crimson under his sparse sandy hair.

"It doesn't matter," Lukas assured him. "We'd like to see the quarry, anyway. Is there a road?"

"Of course. Of course." The man moved to a map tacked to the wall. "You follow this street—"

"We'll find it." Lukas pulled the map they'd taken from Gerry's room out of his jacket pocket. "I've got a map."

All the florid color drained out of the young man's face, and he became noticeably nervous, baffling Nadia.

"Well, then you know where to go, don't you?" he said, attempting a sickly smile.

"What was that all about?" Nadia demanded in frustration when they were once more on the street. Not knowing the language irked her more with every passing hour.

Lukas shrugged, leading her briskly back toward the village square. "The constable is at the quarry. Handy for us. Two jobs done at once."

"That man looked sick, scared or something, when you produced Gerry's map. What's the matter with the people here? The coffee shop owner who doesn't talk, the people who walk by us as if they don't see us." This morning they had passed more black-clad women and men, again going to the church. As yesterday, they had hurried past with averted eyes. "Now this man. Are they hiding something? But that's ridiculous."

"Maybe not, Nadia. There's something going on here. But don't fret, we'll try to find what it is."

"Or die trying," Nadia said with unaccustomed gloominess as they passed the church, which today was decked out in black and deep purple bunting.

They struggled up the rough and steep quarry road. Once they were almost forced off the edge as a truck loaded with an enormous block of marble crept by them, groaning in its low gear.

They crested a hill and the quarry came into view: a huge hole in a barren mountainside flanked by a rusted power shovel and a bulldozer. Yes, Nadia could see that many aspects of the operation could use an efficiency expert, but it didn't seem large enough to warrant the interest of a company like E.C.I.

More and more she was getting the feeling that Gerry had come here for an entirely different reason. She peered into the quarry and recognized the village constable in the clustered group of workmen by his olive uniform. Lukas parked the car next to a dusty row of other vehicles, including a closed-up Jeep bearing the insignia of the police department.

"Wait for me here, Nadia. I shouldn't be long."

She was about to protest, but remembered her ignorance of the language. There wasn't much point in going, if Lukas wouldn't take time to translate. She nodded. "Fine."

He locked the car door, walking away with that loose-limbed stride that made her heart beat a little faster. Last night they had been so close. Today he was all business, an attitude she respected. The faster they cleared this up, the faster they would be free to leave this barren place. And justice would be done if they found Gerry's killer.

Lulled by the warm sun streaming in through the open car window, she leaned her head back against the seat. Closing her eyes, she had almost dozed off when she felt something touch her bare arm, where it rested on the window ledge. Dry, cool, like a bony claw.

She looked down, her mouth dropping open. Only her powerful self-control stifled the scream that rose in her throat. The roar of the machinery faded into the distance as she took in the apparition that crouched on the ground next to the car door.

Chapter Eleven

After her initial shock had faded, Nadia saw that the apparition was a woman, but she looked like a skeleton draped in black. Her skin was a parchment-thin network of wrinkles stretched over a bony facial structure that gave her nose a hawklike prominence. The dark woolen scarf pulled low over her forehead masked the upper part of her face, but Nadia had an impression of rheumy gray eyes framed by thick lashes.

"Come with me," the woman said in a thin cracked voice.

Nadia stifled an urge to laugh. Wasn't that what the witch said to Hansel and Gretel? Then her mouth dropped open as she realized the woman had spoken in English.

"Come with you? Where?" she asked.

The old woman looked blank, then repeated, "Come. You must come." The thready voice held unmistakable urgency.

Nadia looked down into the quarry. Lukas had joined the group of men that included Constable Demos. They seemed to be arguing, abrupt arm gestures punctuating their speech. As she watched they moved farther away, toward a small stone shed, probably the project office, since telephone and power lines fed into it.

She glanced at the old woman, whose clawlike hand still rested on her arm. "Come. Gerald Parker," Nadia heard her say.

The English words were cloaked in a heavy accent, but Nadia had no trouble recognizing her brother's name. "Gerald? You know something about him?"

The woman gestured with her free hand, describing an arc that included the brooding mountain peaks that rose to the north of the village. "Go there."

What did she mean? Did someone have information about Gerald? Hope rebounded in her. Perhaps her journey would bear fruit, after all.

She had to know.

Lukas had told her to wait, but she couldn't ignore the woman's persistent tugging on her arm. Nadia pushed open the car door.

The woman let go of her arm. "Yes." She nodded, the fringe on her scarf swaying. "Come."

Standing on the ground, the car door closed, Nadia again hesitated, thinking of Halias last night. She wasn't about to walk into a trap, was she?

And if she wasn't back soon, how would Lukas know where she'd gone? At the same time, this might be an important lead.

She compromised by pulling a notepad from her purse and scribbling a couple of lines on a sheet torn from it. "Lukas, I'll be back soon. Wait for me."

She laid it on the little ledge in front of the steering wheel, where it would readily be seen. Turning to the old woman, she nodded. "Okay, where do we go?"

The woman set off down a narrow rocky path that led away from the quarry. After about two hundred meters Nadia began to have second thoughts. As if she felt Nadia's doubts, the woman turned her head. She made a sign with her thumb and forefinger, brushing the thumb over the middle knuckle.

Nadia understood the gesture. Half of something. But half of what? Half a minute? Half a mile?

She decided she would give her another couple of minutes, then she would go back and get Lukas.

The path turned sharply back on itself, terminating in a dense clump of trees.

Nadia shivered as they entered the shadowed grove, wishing she hadn't left her sweater in the car. The path led steeply downhill, but only for a short distance, Nadia realized. They hadn't come far from the quarry. She could still hear the sound of the machinery carried on the light wind.

Around her there was silence. No birds sang in the branches, no small creatures rustled in the undergrowth.

The old woman paused, waiting for Nadia to catch up. With one bony finger she pointed to a break in the trees. In the clear area, surrounded by tumbled rocks from an old slide, the dark mouth of a cave stood out, its opening resembling the jaws of some prehistoric beast.

Nadia stopped dead, a chill raising the hairs on her arms. She cursed her vivid imagination, but couldn't shake off a premonition of danger, the feeling that someone was watching her every move.

The old woman grasped her arm with surprising strength. Nadia could still have broken free, but at that moment she heard a sound that made curiosity override apprehension.

Setting all her senses on red alert, she followed the woman inside.

The cave was narrow; Nadia could have touched either wall if she'd stretched out her arms. Muddy spots on the floor squelched under her shoes. The air smelled damp and musty, like the old well she remembered from the country place where they'd lived for several years when she was a girl.

Although the old woman carried no lamp or flashlight, the cavern was not entirely dark. The moss or algae on the slick stone walls glistened with a faint phosphorescent glow, guiding them around difficult bends.

In the distance a light beckoned. Nadia identified the sound that had drawn her into the cave. The rhythmic cadence was louder here, echoing from the stone roof far overhead. It resembled the chanting she'd heard in the village church the evening before.

The passage widened, opening into a circular chamber. Nadia immediately saw what she'd heard. A dozen or so old people stood before an intricately carved icon-covered screen. Illuminated portraits of saints hung on the walls, which were draped in black. At the center of a raised platform stood an enormous painting of Christ being lifted down from the cross. And below that stood a trio of brass stands, tied together with deep purple ribbons and holding scores of votive candles, whose flames flickered eerily across the faces of the worshipers.

A somberly robed priest sang an anthem, to which the people sang a low-voiced refrain. Around him swirled the smoke from his censer, its pungent aroma stinging Nadia's nostrils.

There was an almost pagan quality about this mass, Nadia thought, something alien to her own experience of simple Protestant services. Yet she couldn't deny the power and dignity of it, not its effect on the people, who stood with tears streaming down their lined faces. They mourned for the slain Christ as if he'd been one of their brothers, fathers or sons.

The cold touch of the old woman's hand on her arm drew Nadia's attention away from the ceremony. "Come," she said again in a rasping whisper.

This time Nadia followed with a peculiar sense of fatalism. Whatever was coming, good news or a trap, an inner compulsion drove her on.

They moved only fifty paces down a tunnel so narrow that they had at times to walk sideways. Laying a hand on Nadia's shoulder, the old woman indicated that she should wait. The shuffling of feet continued for a moment, then stopped.

Nadia stood, surrounded by the most profound darkness she'd ever imagined. The air was warm, fetid, like the breath of some wild beast. Here no phosphorescent algae marked the stone wall. There was only deep, depressing night.

A light flared, a guttering torch roughly fashioned from several rags clumped on the end of a stick. The woman held it high, curving her finger to beckon Nadia forward.

Nadia took one step.

And screamed. The shrill cry reverberated in the close air like the echo of a tuning fork.

She was surrounded by skulls, grinning menacingly from decaying wooden shelves fastened to the walls. Below the skulls, boxes of bones stood neatly lined up, with inscriptions marking the names of the deceased scrawled on them.

"No. No," she whispered in horror. Even in a nightmare she'd never seen such a place. She wanted to run, to get to where there was light and sunshine, but her feet seemed rooted to the floor.

The old woman smiled, the gaps between her teeth making her expression a parody of the grinning skulls. "Do not fear," she said, articulating with extreme care. "All dead."

Nadia choked back hysterical laughter. There was truth in her words. They were all dead. They couldn't hurt her.

The woman led her to the corner of the room, where a closed cabinet was crammed between the wooden shelves. "Please," she said, placing the torch in Nadia's hand.

Nadia held the light high as the woman extracted a small key from her pocket. Opening the door of the cabinet, she took an object from the interior. She nodded with evident satisfaction. With another smile she took back the torch and handed the object to Nadia.

Nadia turned over the ordinary, coil-bound notebook in her hands. *Gerald Parker.* The name was written neatly on the cover, along with his Athens address and phone number.

Hardly daring to breathe, she lifted the cover, holding the book nearer the light. To her disappointment the first sheet was blank. Quickly she riffled through the rest of the pages.

At the very end she found it, a loose sheet of unlined paper folded into quarters. Tucking the notebook under her arm, she unfolded the paper.

A map.

She stared at it, her eyes burning from the smoke that was beginning to fill the cavern. Yes, it was of the immediate area, similar to the one she and Lukas had found in Gerald's room. There was the quarry, a circle near the edge of the map. Here was the village in the middle. Even the cave, about halfway between the village and quarry was noted.

On the top corner of the map was an X.

A thin shadow fell across the page as the old woman poked a curved fingernail at the X. "Be careful," she said, her eyes skittering toward the dark reaches of the chamber with its gruesome contents. "Police—not safe. Danger—O Lukas. Be careful."

Nadia's heart leaped into her throat, even as her mind cried out in denial. *No!* It couldn't be!

The darkness enveloped her like a suffocating, malodorous shroud. Heart pounding, her lungs straining for air more out of fear than anything else, she jerked up her head. Had she heard aright?

The woman was gone, melting into the shadows with no more substance than a ghost. She had taken the torch, and Nadia was confronted with the darkness alone. Fortunately she could locate the entrance to the narrow tunnel by the glow of the flickering candles in the chapel. She groped her way down toward the light.

The scene looked as it had before, except that the chanting had become louder as the service climaxed. The smell of incense was hot, heavy, making it difficult to breathe.

Running wasn't possible with the slippery floor of the cave shifting treacherously underfoot. Looking back as if a demon was chasing her, Nadia slipped and slid down the passage to the entrance of the cave.

When she emerged into the grove of trees, she almost drowned in her relief. Nothing had changed in the outside world. The day was warm, the sun shone from a cloudless sky, and birds sang among the leaves. She inhaled deeply, light-headed with the excess oxygen she took in. She knew exactly how Persephone must have felt when she emerged onto the surface of the earth after her prescribed six months in the underworld.

But her relief drained away as she hurried through the grove.

What had the woman said? Was she supposed to be careful of any policeman? Including Lukas?

It couldn't be. Yet she could have sworn that was the name the woman had spoken before she disappeared.

SHE RAN UP THE PATH toward the quarry, sweat forming a film on her face as the sun beat down on her. Wiping at her forehead with the back of one hand, she glanced at the cobalt sky. It had no right to be so hot in April.

The car stood where she had left it. No sign of Lukas. She scanned the quarry, noting that the machinery was still working. Men, looking as small as ants, swarmed over the face of a rock wall, setting explosives, she assumed, to blast down more of the pale veined marble.

She started toward the stone shed, her feet kicking up little puffs of white dust. Almost at the door, she stopped to survey the thickly treed mountain above the quarry.

A glint of light flashed in a split second. She squinted, eyes narrowed as she strained to see against the sun's glare. Had she imagined it? Remembering Halias with his rifle last night, she sprang forward into the shadow of the shed.

From that dubious shelter, her eyes again raked the mountain slopes. Nothing. No movement in the trees, no sign of life other than the shouts and movements of the workmen in the quarry. Even the sky was empty except for a wide-winged hawk floating on air currents at the zenith.

Shaking her head, she grasped the handle of the crude plank door. Maybe it had been nothing. Or only the sun sparkling on broken glass.

Lukas was the only occupant of the shed, sitting in a chair with his feet up on the desk, as if he belonged there. He had the receiver of the telephone pressed to his ear, and from time to time he shouted something incomprehensible into it. *Must be a bad line,* Nadia thought, wondering if it was Gabriel on the other end.

If he was surprised at Nadia's unceremonious entry, when he'd told her to stay in the car, he didn't show it. Waving his hand, he indicated another chair against the wall.

She sat down, her mind turning over the doubts and questions the old woman had raised. Outside, the blast of a warning horn cut across the rumble of the machinery, but Nadia in her concentration barely heard it.

She could trust Lukas, right?

Then again, Lukas was a Greek; she was a stranger, and perhaps a nuisance in this situation.

No. That couldn't be true. Lukas had integrity. He wanted to solve this case as badly as she did.

Lukas had loved her so gently last night. Surely that meant something. But her practical self, wounded by Dorian's duplicity, warned her it might have meant nothing more than the need for human closeness.

The old woman's warning, even if it did not apply to Lukas, was worth heeding. At least until she found out where the map led, and discovered exactly what was going on around here.

Lukas, with a final remark and an abrupt *Antío*, slammed down the receiver. He fixed her with a look that contained no hint of affection, no recollection of the closeness they'd shared.

Nadia shivered. Suddenly she saw either the policeman who was on the trail of a killer, or an enemy. She couldn't tell which. Her hands began to sweat on the laminated cover of the notebook.

"What's that?" Lukas asked.

Silently she handed it over. He turned the pages, every one individually, while she waited. The tension in the room grew, magnified by the heat and dust that seemed to seep through every crack. She shifted nervously on the hard chair, then grew still, praying he hadn't heard the crackle of the map she carried in her back pocket.

"There's nothing here." He looked at her, but she staunchly ignored the accusation in the amber eyes. "Where did you get it?"

There was no point in hiding it from him. As long as he didn't know about the map. "In a cave near here." She shuddered. "It was full of skulls."

Lukas smiled faintly, the harsh lines of his face softening for an instant. "The monks' crypt. It dates back to before the Turkish occupation." The smile faded and he was all business again. "How did you happen to go there? I thought you were to wait in the car."

Briefly she explained about the old woman, the chapel. When she finished, Lukas was scowling. "It could have been a trap, Nadia. You took a very foolish chance."

She lifted her chin defiantly, her temper rising. "I survived it, didn't I?"

He lowered his feet to the floor, placing his elbows on the desk and steepling his fingers before his nose. "Nadia," he said after a moment. "There's a bus out of here at four forty-five this afternoon. I want you on it. You can wait for me in Ioannina." His voice was colder than an Arctic wind, quite an accomplishment, considering the temperature of the room they sat in. A second blast from the horn echoed off the mountains.

Nadia stood up. "Haven't we been through this already? I told you before, and I'm telling you again, I'm staying."

His eyes glittered dangerously as he also got to his feet. "I could have you arrested and thrown into the local jail."

"You mean there is one?" she sneered, so angry she could barely speak. "Just try and get me into it. I'll fight you."

He advanced toward her, circling the desk. Whether he would have picked her up bodily and deposited her in the jail she was never to know. All at once the shed began to tremble violently as an earsplitting sound louder than a typhoon rolled over them. Lukas shouted something that was swallowed up in the roar, then pulled Nadia to him, throwing her to the floor.

It was over in a moment, except for the layer of dust that coated them.

Coughing and retching, they scrambled to their feet, pushing open the door of the shed. Outside, even thicker clouds of dust slowly settled. The power shovel was already eating at the great blocks of marble blasted from the rock face, loading them on waiting trucks.

"Let's go," Lukas said grimly. He herded her none too gently across the quarry to the parking lot. *Damn it,* he had to get her out of here. This case was turning out to be much bigger than anyone could have anticipated.

The attempts on their lives, which he was convinced had been warnings so far, would probably become real very soon. They were getting close to something. The phone call to Gabriel had brought answers to a number of questions. Halias had often been to see Paros in his Athens office. Gabriel's investigations confirmed it. Halias, and very likely Paros too, were criminals who killed people for money, for expedience, for no reason at all. And Lukas had no doubt that either of them would do anything to save his neck.

When he thought of Nadia running around after an old woman, leaving the car and his protection, his blood turned to ice—when it wasn't boiling. He wanted to shake her. He wanted to kiss her. He wanted her gone from here until he arrested Paros and Halias and locked them in prison, preferably in an impenetrable dungeon.

His head was beginning to ache again.

Automatically he walked around the car before getting into it, checking for any irregularities. Nadia waited until he completed the inspection, for once not arguing with him. Although he thought her expression was stubborn, even mutinous, he ignored her temper. It was his job to look for criminals, not hers. She shouldn't be here at all.

They drove back to the village in a tense silence. The streets were still deserted, shrouded in mourning. The church bell tolled continuously, and at intervals the priest and cantors sang out.

Only the blue sky overhead, the pink and white perfection of blooming apple trees, and the warmth of the sun seemed at odds with the intense atmosphere.

"We'll get some bread and cheese and whatever fruit is available at the grocery store," Lukas said. "That'll do for lunch. Nothing else is open today."

"They're working at the quarry," Nadia pointed out.

"Deadlines. This is a big boost to the area's economy. They're doing their best to make sure it continues."

"They're pretty efficient on their own, aren't they?"

"Looks that way," Lukas said. "Are you sure nothing in the letter Gerald sent you gave a hint of what else he might have been up to here?"

Nadia shook her head, the wind catching a strand of her hair and whipping it across her face. Absently she brushed it back, tucking it behind her ear. "No, nothing. I've thought and thought about it."

Lukas stared at her, his heart aching with the need to touch her. The high color in her cheeks, the golden profusion of her hair catching the light, the indomitable spirit that shone from the clear blue of her eyes—he wanted her. He wanted their relationship to last beyond these few days.

Resolutely he cut off his thoughts. It couldn't be. No use crying for an unattainable dream.

They ate their lunch in the grassy yard of an abandoned house. Clover flowers gave off a sweet perfume that jarred with the reality of criminals, guns and danger. A willow, its boughs gracefully hung with delicate new leaves, sheltered them in a hollow that was invisible from passersby.

Lukas welcomed the respite. Out in the open he had been constantly on the alert. He didn't think their enemy had given up. In the light of his talk with Gabriel and the attempts to scare him and Nadia off, he could reach no other conclusion than that Halias and Paros were connected. Although he didn't expect either of them to commit murder in broad daylight, there was no telling what they would do if they became desperate. And he couldn't get rid of the feeling that someone was monitoring his and Nadia's every move. After buying food they had slipped out the back door of the store, threading their way down a goat path between weathered stone buildings. Their present haven seemed safe enough. No one could know where they were.

"Nadia, I want you to go," he said into the silence that surrounded them after they had eaten. During the meal Nadia had been withdrawn, apparently lost in thought. They'd talked little. But now he had to make clear to her the danger she—and he, though it was part of his job—were in.

"It's not because I think you'll be underfoot," he explained, rushing his words. "In fact, you've been a big help. But if everything goes according to plan, all hell will break loose here soon. I don't want you caught in the cross fire."

Nadia gathered up the papers from the cheese and bread, and stuffed them along with the chewed apple cores into the plastic bag they'd carried them in. She had to stay, to follow the clues her instincts told her were valid. Her lips set stubbornly, she avoided his eyes. Lies and subterfuge were so foreign to her that she was sure he would be able to read them all over her face.

"What plan?" She wanted to keep him talking. It kept her from thinking and quaking at the magnitude of her own half-formed plans.

She wished she could confide in him about the map, but as long as she wasn't sure if the woman's warning had been about Lukas, her only hope was to discover the truth about Gerald. She would sort Lukas out later.

"Gabriel finally got some information on Paros," Lukas said, mercifully interrupting her speculations. He let out his breath in a sharp gust. "All of it's bad, so bad that he warned me to be careful, to wait for the men he's sending in." His smile was rueful. "Usually he trusts me to use my best judgment."

"So what's the story on Andreas Paros?" Nadia caught the note of excitement in his tone, the energy that seized a soldier going into battle. But somehow she felt detached, as if it couldn't touch her. Perhaps Paros had done some terrible things during the war, but any man who had married her very ordinary mother couldn't be truly evil.

"He's listed as wanted by Interpol and a score of other countries' police forces, the FBI and the CIA."

It still didn't hit her. "All for shipping children out of Greece nearly forty years ago? Not that that isn't awful—" She shuddered again, the sun failing to burn away the cold dread that settled over her as she recalled the wailing in the island monastery.

"That was the beginning," Lukas stated. "Since then Andreas Paros has done more than almost anyone to undermine world peace. He's among the biggest arms dealers there are."

A hollow chill bored its way through Nadia's stomach. This put a completely different complexion on things. She suddenly realized how irresponsible her plan to confront Paros about Gerry was. She had pictured an old man, embittered by his ostracism, wasted by years of living with the burden of guilt for war crimes on his shoulders. She could have walked right into this conscienceless criminal's lair, if indeed the mark on the map indicated his hideout. But why else would Gerry have marked the spot?

She had to tell Lukas, to let him make a plan more practical than her harebrained scheme. The words hovered on the tip of her tongue. But she bit them back as the woman's muttered words rang again in her head. *Danger. O Lukas. Be careful.*

"Are you saying that Sally was right, that he killed Gerry? His own son?" She was proud her voice didn't waver.

"I've got people still checking on Gerry's background. Nadia, they keep coming up against classified files. That worries me. In itself it indicates Gerry wasn't who he appeared to be. I think he came up here specifically to find Paros—but not as a son looking for his father."

"What are you saying? That my brother was some sort of undercover agent?" she burst out.

Lukas sighed, framing his words carefully. "I'm afraid so, Nadia. My police sources have run down some of the places Gerry's been in the past ten years. In the majority of cases there was what you might call an incident involving arms dealers, terrorists and others of that type. It's impossible to dismiss his presence there as a coincidence. And the classified files are a giveaway he's under some government protection."

Nadia's head reeled. *Gerry?* It couldn't be. Yet now that she thought back, it was a logical explanation for certain aspects of his life. He was vague about his job. He traveled a lot. He rarely brought back photographs. He had few friends and only superficial involvements with women. Much as she hated to admit it, Lukas's explanation did answer more questions than it asked.

"And Paros found out he was going to visit him and had him killed," she mused, black depression clutching her heart. A man who killed his own son was capable of any kind of atrocity.

"Wait," Lukas said. "That's where it gets really interesting. According to some of the workers at the quarry, a man answering to Gerry's description has been seen in the mountains since his funeral."

Nadia's mouth dropped open. "What?" She grabbed Lukas by the shoulders, nearly upsetting him in her excitement. "Are you sure? Where is he, and why hasn't he tried to contact us?" Her eyes shone as she jumped to her feet. "Lukas, do you realize what this could mean? He's alive!"

Lukas also got up. "Don't pin your hopes too high. It's only a rumor. When I tried to question the man, he changed the subject, looked around as if he were scared someone would overhear."

Nadia sobered. *Like the old woman with her warnings.* Rumors. Speculations. What did the X on the map mean? She had to find out, on her own. If she showed Lukas the map, he would take it—and send her to Ioannina, anyway.

"It may not be true at all," Lukas said. "But it's certainly something to keep in mind. After all, his men arranged the burial and the coffin was closed. If the villagers suspected anything unusual at the funeral, they're not talking about it. And if Gerry's alive, it could explain why we received so little information on the case."

"But they were sending you here to investigate." Nadia frowned.

"'They' are my police department and the Canadian Embassy. The secret services don't confide in those organizations. Eventually we'd learn something didn't ring right, what with those classified files and all. But they'd have bought the time they needed."

Was that true? Nadia wondered. Or was it another seemingly logical excuse to keep her from digging too deeply? "How do I know that?" she asked coldly. "You could have been assigned to see that I didn't come too close to the truth. Would we ever have known, or would the funeral have been the end of it? If Gerry is alive—still a big 'if'—will we see him again, or will his organization bury him figuratively, as well?"

"I don't know. I don't even know who he's working for, and they're not likely to confide in me, either. But I would imagine that as soon as they finish with Paros, Gerry will be as free as he ever was."

"If this Paros is such a noted criminal, how is it that he's been at liberty for so long?"

"He's an expert at covering his tracks, always has a perfect alibi. But apparently someone found out something. Perhaps success made him careless. But you can bet he won't be careless again." He took Nadia's hands in his, noting how icy her fingers were. "Nadia, you see why you must go. You might be next."

In spite of her doubts, she heard the gentleness in his voice, felt the warmth of his hands, as if he held her heart.

And he did, didn't he? For the first time in her life she understood how a woman could remain loyal to her man, even after she discovered the most heinous things about him. No matter what Lukas was, she had lost her heart to him, almost from the moment his golden eyes had met hers in the crowded airport. Jet lag wasn't affecting her judgment now.

She wanted to do as he said. She didn't want to defy him. But there were too many things that didn't add up. She couldn't leave it to him. She had to be sure nothing went wrong.

She looked at him. He waited. Slowly, regretfully she shook her head. "I have to stay."

The silence stretched, bleak and ugly. Around them bees burrowed into clover flowers, releasing the fragrance into the still air. Lukas shrugged, his face hard, expressionless. "As you wish, but I can't be responsible for what happens." He picked up the bottle that had held their water. "Want another drink?"

"It's empty." Nadia could hardly speak around the thickness in her throat.

"I'll fill it. I saw a pump just on the other side of the abandoned house." He glanced around the overgrown yard. "There's only one way in here. You'll be safe enough for a minute," he added, almost as if to contradict himself.

He disappeared between the dusty stone walls. Nadia watched him go, his limber stride covering the ground with a smooth economy of effort. Briefly she closed her eyes. She hated deceiving Lukas, but she just couldn't be sure he wasn't deceiving her. The revelation about Paros, the imminent arrival of reinforcements for Lukas, and his renewed efforts to get her out of the way might, after all, be as they appeared on the surface.

Or they might be the steps leading to a discreet expulsion of the criminal from the country. Greece had been accused often enough in recent years of providing a safe haven for displaced persons with questionable reputations. News of Paros's arrest would hit the press with banner headlines, and provide more fuel for bad publicity.

The longer she thought about it, a whitewash of the situation seemed more likely.

Could Lukas be part of that? It made her feel sick to consider it, but she concluded he could. His first loyalty would be to his country and his duty, not to her.

She got up, restlessly stepping out of the shelter of the willow boughs. Should she try to give him the slip? *Could* she? If she climbed over the stone wall at the far end of the yard, she might be able to squeeze between two warehouse walls to freedom.

A pebble landed beside her. She jumped, her heart rebounding crazily in her chest. She looked around. Nothing. A bird in the willow set up an ecstatic warbling, and the sun poured down on her.

She uttered a quiet laugh that held no humor. The tension and isolation were getting to her.

The bird broke off in midnote.

A faint sound brought Nadia's glance up, and a scream caught, stillborn, in her throat.

From the roof of the vacant house, a heavy clay tile hurtled down toward her.

Chapter Twelve

Using reflexes she'd never known she had, Nadia flung herself to one side. The tile swept by to smash into jagged shards on the hard ground.

Her hands at her throat, Nadia stood frozen. Her breath rasped with raw violence in her chest. She raked her burning eyes over the roof but saw no one, heard nothing except the wind stirring the top of the willow.

"Nadia, I couldn't get the damn thing working."

She started at the sound of Lukas's voice. Quickly she stepped away from the shattered clay, realizing that the pieces were nearly invisible in the tall weeds.

Bending to pick up the plastic bag that held the remains of their lunch, she fought against nausea. *Lukas.* He could have done it. He'd been gone long enough and he was agile enough to climb onto the roof of the single-story building.

She stifled a moan. *No.* It couldn't be. The idea that Lukas had tried to kill her was so repugnant that she couldn't grasp it. But he wanted her to go. He might have gone this far to scare her.

"Lukas, you win." To her own ears her voice sounded faint and thready. "I'll go." She had to convince him she meant it, in order to get away from him long enough to follow the markings on the map. If Gerry was alive, she would find him.

Lukas stared at her, his relief like a bubble of helium in his chest.

"I'm glad," he said, stepping toward her.

She jerked back, as if she'd touched a hot stove. "I hope you're happy."

Something was wrong. Lukas's eyes narrowed. She was pale, agitated. His foot crunched on something in the grass and he looked down. Chunks of clay littered the ground.

"Nadia, what happened?"

She lifted her head, her eyes glistening with tears. "You didn't have to go that far. I could have been killed."

He grabbed her arm with ungentle fingers, a sinking feeling in his stomach. His body felt as if he'd plunged it into ice water. "Nadia!"

Shaking free, she started toward the path that led out of the suddenly claustrophobic enclosure. "A roof tile nearly hit me."

"And you think I did it." His voice was all the more terrible for its faintness.

"Who else could have?"

Anyone else, he thought, but he said nothing, the tearing pain of her distrust making words die unspoken.

Single file, with Nadia in the lead, they moved up the narrow path to emerge onto the street. Expecting to find it deserted, Nadia was shocked to see the skeletal form dressed in black, half-hidden in a doorway.

"That's her." She leaped forward at a run, but the woman moved at the same instant, pausing only to throw two words over her shoulder.

"Danger. Danger."

She hesitated another moment, looking past Nadia at Lukas, who had just stepped free of the shadowed passage. The clawlike hand lifted, the bony finger pointing. "Be careful."

Nadia stopped in confusion. Was the warning directed at her, about Lukas? Or was it meant for Lukas himself?

"Well, get after her," she cried. The old woman, black skirts flapping, had vanished into a narrow valley between two buildings.

"It's too late," he said. "We'll never find her in that maze." He looked at his watch. "Besides, we can't take the time. You have to catch that bus."

They started off down the street in a heavy silence. The coffee shop was in sight when Lukas finally spoke. "You're wrong, you know, Nadia," he said tightly, his mouth drawn into a thin line. "If I'd wanted you hurt, I didn't have to lift a finger. I could have given Halias any number of opportunities. If you think about it, you'll know I didn't try to kill you."

"Somebody did." She sounded sure, but deep inside, doubts sprang to life. "Oh, Lukas, I just don't know what to believe anymore. Strange things have been happening all along. Maybe it's this place."

"Maybe." He pulled in a deep breath. "Nadia, I thought you trusted me."

"I don't know who to trust anymore. All these warnings."

Startled, he turned his head toward her. "Warnings? Have there been others?"

Now she'd done it. "It doesn't matter. I'm going." *But not to Ioannina.* What would she find at the place marked on the map? Gerry, or more danger? No matter; she had to pursue it.

She could feel Lukas's perplexity change to frustration, as she determinedly kept a distance between them. The church bell, which had been silent since noon, began again, its sonorous refrain following them down the street.

The coffee shop was unlocked when they arrived, but the rush-seated chairs were upended on the tables. Even their landlord had apparently abandoned his business in the absence of customers.

Nadia headed for the washroom next to the stairs, ignoring Lukas's increasing impatience. "Could you wait a minute? I'd like to wash my face and comb my hair first."

How was she going to escape his protective custody? Nadia wondered a short time later, as she methodically repacked the few items she'd taken out of her suitcase last night. Lukas prowled around the room, tense and impatient as an expectant father. At intervals he stared out of the window at the mountains that ringed the village.

Was someone watching them, even now penetrating the glass with binoculars? He scowled at the trees that provided plenty of cover. To his relief he'd had no sense that anyone had been stalking them. But he couldn't shake off his uneasiness, the sensation that something wasn't right.

Someone had tried either to kill Nadia or scare her badly. At least it had had the positive effect of making her finally agree to leave. She would be safe.

Or would she? All at once he wondered if his indefinable anxiety involved her. Was it a presentiment of further danger? That old woman— He had to find her, question her, but first he had to get rid of Nadia.

He raked his fingers through his hair, his eyes unseeing on the horizon. It must be something else. The snapping of her suitcase locks made him spin around.

"Okay, Nadia, spit it out." His voice sliced harshly through the silence. "You don't still think I dropped the tile, do you? I'll prove it to you, I'm on your side. I'll find Paros, and Gerry too, if he's alive. You'll see."

"It isn't that." Nadia's thoughts skittered in alarm, but the idea that she was in danger from Lukas had faded into the background, superceded by the more immediate prospect of following the map. And the possible danger of such a move. "I'm just disappointed that the woman ran off." She couldn't let him suspect anything now.

She smiled, feeling as if her face were cracking under the falseness of it. Softly she crossed the floor, laying a hand on his cheekbone, touching the edge of the bandage. "Are you all right, Lukas? Does your head hurt? You've been running around, exerting yourself. You should have been resting."

"My head is okay." He shook it impatiently, his cop's instincts fighting with the desire to hold her once more. Something was wrong. Warnings twisted in his gut. If only he could put his finger on it.

Her scent, something woodsy and mossy today, like spring in a deep forest, traveled to him. He inhaled, imprinting it into his brain, a tactile reminder of her.

Against his will, his eyes strayed to the rumpled bed, picturing Nadia in it, wishing they had more time. Why did he feel as if the moment they left this room he would never see her again? He was going crazy. Was there something in the village that blighted lives, annihilating hope?

He shook his head again, taking her suitcase from her hand. She glanced around the room, checking to see if she'd forgotten anything. Her brow creased in a frown. "Where's my purse?"

"I don't have it." Lukas sounded irritated. "What would I do with a woman's purse? Maybe you left it downstairs."

Her brow cleared. "Yes, I must have." She remembered now. She'd set it on the bar while she went over to the telephone. She'd briefly entertained the idea of phoning somewhere to confirm what Lukas had told her this afternoon. But not only did she have no idea whom to phone, but the phone turned out to have one of those ingenious locks that prevented unauthorized use.

She went down the stairs ahead of him. *Yes.* There it was, lying on the bar. She picked it up, clutching it quickly when the flap opened and the contents almost spilled out.

Strange. She was sure she'd fastened it after she'd combed her hair. Setting it on the bar, she stuffed her wallet, checkbook and assorted other items back into place. Lukas tapped his foot as he waited by the door, scowling. "Come on, will you?"

She was about to snap back at him when the corner of a white paper sticking out of the checkbook folder caught her eye. "Wait a minute. I think I have to go to the bathroom."

Lukas rolled his eyes toward the ceiling. "You just went."

But she didn't hear him as she slammed the door.

Hands shaking, she pulled out the small note. "Nadia," it said. "I am in trouble. Come. Tell no one." It was signed "Gerry." She stared at the scrawled words. Was it his handwriting? His signature looked real, but she couldn't be sure. He'd always typed his letters to her.

"Nadia, let's move." The irritation in Lukas's voice overrode her thoughts.

Stuffing the note into her purse, she came out, her face composed in what she hoped was a neutral expression. Behind the calm facade, her mind worked overtime. Maybe she had been wrong. Maybe the X on the map indicated Gerry's hiding place. At the time she had thought he was dead, but if he was alive, it made sense.

Probably aware that she was leaving, someone had managed to slip the note into her purse. Someone sent by Gerry. There was no other explanation. Gerry needed her. He might be hurt. She had to go.

Tell no one. Did that include Lukas? *Yes.* Especially in view of what had happened, she had to assume it did.

THE BUS STOP, a lean-to, made of stone with a sheet metal roof and a wooden bench along each side stood opposite the village office and police station. To Nadia's frustration Lukas stayed right beside her until the bus, spewing dense black diesel fumes, groaned to a stop. He waited until a couple of old men creaked arthritically down the steps. With a brief word to the driver he got on, stowing Nadia's case in the overhead rack before extracting a couple of bills from his wallet. Ignoring her protest, he paid for the ticket and handed her the cardboard token.

He accompanied her to an empty seat. "Here you are, Nadia." He hesitated, his eyes locked with hers, communicating the unspoken emotions in his heart. "You'll wait for me in Ioannina, won't you? I'll be along to pick you up. We'll drive back to Athens together.

"Nadia," he pleaded when she remained silent, staring at him with those troubled blue eyes. "Give us a chance—a chance to know each other when there's nobody chasing us. I'll be there or I'll send word to you no later than Sunday night." Disregarding the unwinking stares of the half dozen or so passengers and the bus driver, who was watching them in the rearview mirror, he planted a long, hard kiss on her mouth. "Until then."

Halfway down the aisle, he turned. "Give my mother a call, will you? Tell her we'll be home in the early part of the week." He lifted his hand in a parting salute. "Take care, Nadia."

Sorrow and guilt burdened her. "You too, Lukas," she whispered belatedly as he vaulted off the bus. Unconsciously she touched a fingertip to her lips, more to savor than to soothe the tingling heat left by his kiss.

Turning toward the window as the driver engaged the gears and sent the ungainly vehicle lurching onto the road, she craned to see Lukas. His arms crossed on his chest as he gazed after the bus, he appeared an isolated figure against the massive bulk of the mountains.

With a forced smile she wasn't sure he could see through the dusty glass, she waved. As the bus rounded the first curve in the road, he lifted his hand and waved back.

Nadia slumped down in the seat, thinking rapidly. She had to get off the bus, before it went too far from the village. It could be a problem, if Lukas had given the driver instructions to keep an eye on her all the way to Ioannina.

Inclining her head over the aisle between the seats she studied the road ahead. Two curves and the beginning of the upward grade. If she remembered their arrival, there was a bus stop on the brief level stretch before the long climb out of the valley.

If she could get off there—

She pulled her suitcase from the luggage rack. It would encumber her, but the driver would think it strange if she left it behind. She struggled to the front of the bus, fighting to keep her balance as the driver swerved abruptly to avoid a pothole.

"Excuse me," she began, then cleared her throat as she realize the tentative tone was not audible above the roar of the diesel engine.

"Stop the bus," she said loudly. "I must go back. I forgot something important."

The driver paid no attention, probably not understanding English. Stepping on the clutch he shifted to a lower gear, the overworked transmission grinding in earsplitting protest. Nadia clenched her teeth in frustration.

The bus rounded the second curve. It was nearly at the stop. No one stood there. No one on the bus had signaled that they wanted to get off, putting an end to any possibility that she could simply jump off when it stopped.

Then she had an inspiration as the mad swaying of the bus, amplified by her upright position, produced a discomfort in her stomach she hardly had to fake.

"Stop the bus," she yelled. To emphasize her words she pushed her face next to the driver's and clamped her hand over her mouth.

Brakes shrieking, he slammed to a stop, the doors flapping open. With a jaunty wave, Nadia hopped off. *"Antío. Antío."* She repeated her farewell twice for good measure, hoping he would get the message.

Apparently he did, for the doors closed with a rubbery slap, and the bus jerked back into motion to continue its laborious journey up the slope. Nadia waited until it vanished around the next curve, leaving behind only the gray pall of its pungent exhaust.

THE FLAT GREEN EYES stared through the binoculars, noting the lonely figure of the woman, her pale shirt a beacon in the gathering dusk. The plan was working. She hadn't gone meekly back to Ioannina. A willful woman. It might be pleasant to experiment a little with the endurance of that spirit before he got rid of her. *Yes.* Very pleasant indeed.

The man's lips pulled back from his teeth in a cruel parody of a smile. "Go, little pigeon. Into the net."

NADIA LOOKED AROUND, taking a moment to reconnoiter and to plan what she would do next.

Next to the bus stop sign, a faint path led into the scrub. A goat path, or a trail used by people? The map might tell her.

She walked up the path until she was hidden from the road. Sitting down on a boulder, she pulled the map from her pocket. Luckily it was still there. After her picnic with Lukas and the leap to escape the falling tile, she wouldn't have been surprised if she'd lost it.

Yes. There were the road and the bus stop. She was on the right path. How far? She stared at the sky. The evenings were long, but the bus had been late. As on the evening they'd spent on Atalanti, storm clouds were gathering in the west. The sun rested almost on top of them, lighting the ragged edges. The strong wind meant they wouldn't take long to reach her.

It was imperative that she find the place before nightfall. Growing up in Vancouver, she was familiar with reports of lost hikers and the dangers of mountain trails in the dark. She had no desire to stumble over a cliff. She knew her limitations. She was a runner, at home on level cinder paths, not mountain tracks.

The suitcase would slow her down. She opened it and took out the short down ski jacket she hadn't needed before. The sun was still warm, but as soon as it slid behind the clouds, the evening would turn chilly. April at this altitude was not summer, no matter how much she'd sweated during the day.

After putting a change of underwear into her large purse, she stashed the case behind the boulder, marking its location in her head for future reference. Swinging her purse over her shoulder, she set off.

What would she find at her destination? A wounded Gerry? He must be unable to travel or he would have come to her himself.

Unless he was hiding from Paros. Initially she had been inclined to dismiss Sally's statement that Paros could have killed his own son as hysteria. But now that she knew about Paros, conjecture had become a virtual certainty. Paros was capable of anything.

A low rumble of thunder shook the earth. Nadia shivered as a cool wind swept down from the clouds, buffeting her with unexpected force as she crested a ridge. She leaned into the wind, tugging her jacket around her chest and zipping it securely.

She had been walking for more than an hour in the direction indicated by the map. Where was the place? The storm clouds had risen to obscure the sun, lending the remaining daylight a twilight murkiness that filled her with foreboding.

Trudging along a ledge that hung over a deep gorge filled with trees, she berated herself. It was too late to turn back now. She had to continue on the faint path.

The mountains stretched endlessly around her, while intervals of lightning strafed the faraway mauve peaks.

The path widened. Nadia quickened her steps, soon coming out onto a rutted track that cut across a high meadow. Scanning the open ground she looked for any kind of shelter, picturing a small stone hut such as Lukas had pointed out on the road—a place where shepherds lived when they took their flocks into the hills.

But the meadow showed no sign of human presence other than the track. The grass was dotted with poppies, and driven before the wind, became an undulating sea of green and blood red.

At the far side of the meadow the track continued through a gorge barely wide enough for a vehicle to pass through. Then it narrowed further, to become almost a tunnel. Through a thin crack in the rocks overhead Nadia could see only a sliver of sky. The wind moaned eerily, kicking up whirlwinds of dust.

Then another sound traveled across the desolation, a keening howl that raised the hairs on the back of Nadia's neck.

A wolf. She hadn't imagined it last night. But Lukas had warned her about wild animals in these mountains.

Lukas. She should have told him about the map, asked his advice. She should have disregarded the injunction in the note. This track was too well-used to be going to a shepherd's hut.

An ugly suspicion came to life inside her. Gerry hadn't sent the note at all. She was walking into a trap.

She emerged from the gorge, welcoming the last minutes of daylight. Sunset streaked the clouds with a vivid red as she stumbled into another meadow. Another sea of rippling grass and spring flowers.

But this meadow wasn't deserted. At the far end she saw a rambling stone house, crouching on a knoll. Its gray walls blended with the granite cliffs behind it, as if it had sprung fully fledged from the earth. At one corner a stark tower, with narrow slits for windows, rose four stories into the brooding sky, dwarfed only by the crag that formed a protective fortress at the back of the house.

Nadia stopped, apprehension pressing as heavily upon her as the storm massed overhead. The air was close, despite the wind. She drew in a breath to relieve the tension in her chest. The wind carried the pungent odor of ozone, unrefreshing, oppressive.

A hawk cried raucously, panicking a flock of birds into flight from a copse nearby. Nadia felt their fear.

She could have turned back. She *should* have turned back. But curiosity, and that odd compulsion she'd felt before, drove her forward.

Resolutely denying the possibility of danger, thinking only that Gerry somehow had called her, that he needed her, she started across the meadow.

THE MASSIVE FRONT DOOR of the house had no bell or knocker. When Nadia rapped her fist against the oak panels, the effort was hardly worth the sore knuckles that followed. No one inside could have heard the knock.

She looked about for a stick or a stone to bang with but before she found anything suitable, a carriage lamp next to the door came on, trapping her in a pool of light.

The door opened, swinging wide to reveal a brightly lighted hall. Her heart thudding painfully in her throat, Nadia stepped forward into the light.

She looked up, to find herself staring into a pair of dark blue eyes the exact shade of those that looked back at her from the bathroom mirror every morning. The emptiness in her stomach suddenly lurched and rendered her speechless.

"I was wondering when we would meet." The voice was soft, with a chilling emphasis on the initial consonants. "Good evening, daughter."

Chapter Thirteen

"Come in. Come in," the man continued.

Her brain was numb. There was no way she could send a message to her feet, telling them to run.

This was Andreas Paros, master criminal, man "most wanted" on several continents. A man who lived off the death and misery of other human beings.

What did he mean by "daughter"?

He looked like anyone's idea of a grandfather, strong body still erect despite his age, his handsome, well-preserved face framed by white hair and dominated by those telltale blue eyes.

The eyes were unmistakable. Paul Roberts had brown eyes. Nadia had wondered about the fact that her eyes were identical in color to Gerry's despite her mother's casual dismissal. Sally's eyes were blue also, but a pale translucent shade that bore no resemblance to her children's distinctive color.

Floundering, fighting against the nightmare horror, she tried to deny it. "No, Paul Roberts is my father. You can't be."

"Oh, but I can, dear Nadia. I can." As he spoke he wrapped one hand around her arm, drawing her inside. "Come in. Let me close the door. The night will be cold with the storm coming up. You're not afraid of storms, are you, Nadia?"

Storms? She almost laughed but forced herself not to, in case she couldn't stop. "I'm not afraid of anything," she declared recklessly.

He smiled at her with a chilling display of perfect teeth, like a shark's. Nadia's fingers tightened on her purse strap as she suppressed a shudder. Why hadn't she told Lukas where she was going? He wouldn't even think of her coming here.

"That little woman must have been pregnant when she left," Paros was saying conversationally. "I wonder if she knew. Well, no matter. You're here now. And if I can just find Gerry, the family will be complete."

He's mad, she thought, wondering why she wasn't surprised. The numbness dissipated, leaving her mind lucid, composing the questions for which she needed answers, buying time to work on an escape plan. "I thought Gerry was dead. Isn't that his grave in the village cemetery?"

She saw a childish petulance in the way his mouth turned down. "Yes, of course it is. His name is on it." For a second he seemed confused, a confusion Nadia shared. Were the rumors false? Was Gerry really dead?

She jumped as Paros slammed his right fist into his left palm. "Next time will be different. No mistakes."

"You killed your own child?" She couldn't keep the revulsion from her voice. "I suppose you're also planning to kill me."

The blue eyes were cold and speculative as they rested on her. "No, it might not be necessary. I've never enjoyed killing women, although Kyriakos has."

"What about the roof tile?" It was a stab in the dark, but found its mark.

"That was an accident. Kyriakos was listening to your most informative conversation, and his hand slipped." He smiled thinly. "I'm not going to be here much longer. Too many people know where I am. It's time I changed headquarters. By tomorrow night I'll be gone."

Tomorrow night. Hadn't Lukas said something about tomorrow night? "There are people who know where I am," Nadia said bravely. "They'll be looking for me."

Paros laughed lightly. "Oh, you mean that lovesick fool Stylianos. If he hadn't been so busy looking after you, he would have been more effective in his job." He rubbed one hand over his chin. Nadia noticed his hands were smooth as a woman's, the nails perfectly manicured and glossy with colorless polish. "Yes, that gives me an idea. Stylianos is expecting reinforcements tomorrow. They'll come here. Now, if I send him a message that I've got you, he'll come storming to your rescue. Since he's the only one with any idea where this place is, I'll be well away before any of his associates arrive."

"You're forgetting one thing. Obviously your spies weren't thorough enough. Lukas and I had a fight before I left. He's considering himself well rid of me. He thought me nothing more than a nuisance, all along."

Paros laughed again. He touched her cheek, the soft feel sending a shudder through her body. "That kiss he gave you in the bus wasn't the kind a man would give a woman he considered a nuisance. Don't look surprised. My spies are everywhere. No, Stylianos cares about you. He'll come. All I have to do is let him know you're in trouble."

"You sent the note I thought was from Gerry." Nadia jerked her head back, her skin crawling. "You brought me here."

"I was curious, my dear. It's lonely to live your life without ever knowing your children. I planted the map, as well. Oh, it was Gerry's, but he left some of his personal effects behind when we last met. When I realized Stylianos was bundling you out of town, I had someone put the note into your purse. To convey urgency, you understand. It was very accommodating of you to leave it on the bar, although if necessary I would have used the old woman again."

She'd been manipulated from beginning to end. She felt sick, unable to say anything.

Paros put his hand on her elbow. "Come, my dear. Dinner is waiting."

"The last meal for the condemned woman, I suppose," Nadia said with dry irony.

"Tut, tut," he said. "It won't come to that. You can come with me. I'll guarantee you a life in which you'll want for nothing."

"Only my freedom," she retorted.

"Semantics, my dear. Mere semantics."

He led her down a corridor with a stone floor that was cold and uncarpeted. Dust kittens scurried ahead of them, disturbed by the draft of their passage. The stucco walls were lighted with horizontal lamps, each positioned over a paler square. Nadia was puzzled for a moment, then understood. Paintings had hung on the walls, and had only recently been removed. The meaning of Paros's cryptic remark became clear. He was abandoning the place.

The supposition was confirmed as soon as she entered the room he showed her. "You'll want to freshen up," he said. "There is a bath through that door. I'll be back in, shall we say, ten minutes?"

The room was furnished with a double bed, still made up with sheets and a heavy woolen blanket. In the small bath there were towels and soap, but little else.

Ten minutes, he'd said. Nadia eyed the shower stall, at the same time pulling off her jacket and sweater. She hadn't had a proper bath in days and wasn't about to pass up this opportunity. He would just have to wait. The thought of his impatience pleased her more than she wanted to admit.

She had just finished dressing and was running her brush through her hair when she heard Paros pounding on the door. A glance at her watch told her fifteen minutes had passed. She smiled grimly. Pulling back her towel-dried hair, she began to braid it into a single thick plait.

The door burst open and Paros came in, his mouth set in a grim line. Although her heart quaked, she glared at him in open defiance. "Ten minutes, I said." His voice didn't rise, but the venom in it made her hand shake as she slipped a covered elastic over the end of her braid.

It was then that the first doubt crept into her mind.

Was this man really her father? Could any father reveal such hostility, such hatred to a daughter he'd never seen? Logic, fed by daily newspaper and television reports of child abuse and family violence, told her it was possible. It happened every day in the real world. Yet somehow, something didn't ring true here.

"Dinner is served," he said through clenched teeth, a feat she would have thought impossible.

"Thank you." Gracefully she rose from the edge of the bed, straightening the hem of her sweater with as much care as if it had been a satin gown. She extended her elbow to him. "Shall we go?"

Out of the corner of her eye, she had the satisfaction of seeing him gape and then quickly snap his mouth shut. He took her arm, and if he held it too tightly, Nadia considered it fair payment for successfully throwing him off balance.

The dining room had the same air of imminent desertion as the bedroom and hallways. The walls were bare of pictures, decorated only by small nail holes and pale rectangles. Wide windows, naked of draperies, coldly reflected their images against the black night.

They sat down at a table that was far too small for the cavernous room, on hard rush chairs like those used in common coffee shops. But the cloth was of white linen, and over the table an elaborate chandelier fitted with electric candles refracted a soft light from the glasses filled with a ruby wine.

A stooped old man, his face set in a dour expression, served the soup. Nadia tasted only a couple of spoonfuls. She wouldn't have put it past her captor father to have drugged the food.

When the soup bowls were replaced by plates, and a huge platter appeared, on which rested a beautifully browned leg of lamb, her appetite got the better of her. Hungrily she accepted the succulent slices Paros carved from the roast. He served himself as well, so she figured the meat was all right.

"Not keeping the Holy Week fast, are you?" she asked, breaking the silence that had become oppressive.

He waved his hand, his mouth twisting in a grimace. "Superstitious nonsense." He narrowed his eyes craftily. "However, I can use that superstition to my advantage. Tomorrow night, during the celebration—" He broke off and sipped from his wineglass, wiping his mouth afterward with all the delicacy of a cat. "Yes, that should work very well. An unfortunate accident, no questions or bothersome investigations."

Nadia's mouth grew as dry as dust. She pushed away her plate, the sight of the fat congealing around the remaining pieces of meat making her stomach churn. To settle it, she gulped from her wineglass, welcoming the heady warmth of the alcohol.

She couldn't be the child of this cold-blooded man, who was calmly planning her murder at the dinner table. She stood up, her chair falling to the floor with a clatter.

"Sit down."

His icy voice stung her. Picking up the chair, she sat down again, so abruptly that she bit her tongue. She could taste the salty blood in her mouth.

A sound at the open doorway pulled her gaze from the man's face, where the handsome features no longer hid the evil in his soul.

She saw the intruder and felt her face go still and white.

The animal whose expressionless yellow eyes studied her might have been conjured out of her nightmares. He stood over a meter high at the shoulders, the dark fur overlaid with white, as if covered with hoarfrost. The bushy tail hung low, motionless.

Dogs wagged their tails; wolves did not.

"Ah, there you are, my friend." Paros extended a hand and the wolf came near, sniffing it without taking his eyes from Nadia. The jaws opened and a long black tongue emerged, sliding once over the glistening white fangs, as if he could taste the sweetness of Nadia's flesh.

She sat frozen in her chair. The feral gleam in the wolf's cruel yellow eyes paralyzed her.

The servant came in, silently moving from one place to the other as he cleared the table. "We'll have coffee in my den," Paros said, rising with his hand on the wolf's neck. "Come, Nadia."

As she got up the wolf growled, a deep rumble in its throat. "We're the same, he and I," Paros said blandly. "*Ó Lýkos,* the Wolf, that's what they call me. I strike and then I'm gone, silently, like the hunting wolf. And like the hunting wolf, I've learned to live with solitude. I've even learned to enjoy it."

Ó Lýkos. Nadia felt heat, then cold suffuse her body. That was what the old woman in the cave had said. Not Lukas. The word had been *Lýkos.*

The woman had tried to warn her about Paros, even as she carried out his instructions.

The wolf left Paros's side, coming up to sniff at her thigh. Even through the fabric of her jeans she could feel the hot breath. A gasp escaped her lips as he poked his cold nose against her hand. She yanked it out of danger, but the animal merely yawned, showing long curving fangs set in gums as black as licorice. Nadia had the distinct impression he was toying with her, perhaps even deciding which portion of her anatomy would be most appetizing.

The den—appropriate name, Nadia thought half hysterically—was elegantly appointed, although again blank areas on the walls told her that paintings had been removed. Paros was already packing, preparing to flee. A fire blazed on a massive stone hearth and red velvet draperies gave the room a deceptive air of coziness.

Paros waved her to a leather sofa and, closely attended by the wolf, she sat down. The creature stretched out at her feet, his eyes lambent in the firelight. Although he appeared at rest, she knew he was watching her every move. As long as the beast shadowed her, she would have no chance to escape—no chance to keep Paros in Greece.

On the far side of the room Paros adjusted the dials on a complex of sophisticated electronic equipment. After a moment the strains of Vivaldi emerged from hidden speakers. Violins. *The Four Seasons,* beginning with the stately melodies of "Spring."

Paros moved to the bar in the corner and she had a clear view of the equipment.

Beside the stereo, the bank of shelves contained a computer, the cursor blinking like a lazy emerald eye, and a radiotelephone. *Probably has an independent power source,* she surmised. She knew little about electronics, but was sure that she could use this equipment to call for help.

If she could shake off her captor and the wolf.

Fat chance, she thought as the animal displayed his awesome teeth in another yawn, before settling down with his head on his outstretched paws.

"A brandy, my dear daughter?" Paros asked in the dulcet tones of a perfect host.

"I'm not your daughter," she said mechanically, her eyes still on the equipment.

"Oh, but you are," he said silkily as he handed her the snifter.

"Maybe. But not with my consent," she retorted, her knuckles white against the glass. The brandy shone with an amber glow that reminded her of Lukas's eyes. *Oh, my love, I'm so sorry. I should have trusted you.*

His expression did not alter. He shrugged. "It's of little importance. I've learned to depend on no one but myself. I shall continue to do so."

Nadia drank the liquor, letting the mellow fire slide down her throat. It pooled in her nearly empty stomach, warming the chilly fear that she kept at bay by sheer bravado.

The violins approached a crescendo, their volume and velocity increasing until the music rang in her head. The walls with their crimson hangings pressed in on her. With an effort she focused her eyes on her captor.

"Tell me, where do you get your electricity? A generator? I didn't see any power lines."

"Yes. Although the village is not far, I feel more secure not to have to depend on the public power system. In storms it often fails."

The room was becoming uncomfortably warm. Nadia set down her glass and got to her feet. The wolf rumbled and lifted his head, but at a word from Paros he settled down again.

She was allowed to climb to her room and go to bed. Under the covers she was able to reflect on her dilemma. Obviously Paros meant to keep her alive until tomorrow, or he would have sent her out into the night, accompanied by Halias and his rifle. She would have to look for an avenue of escape. The madman had to be stopped. She would sleep on the problem. Perhaps in daylight, if she had an opportunity to run for it, she stood a better chance of escaping and getting help.

LUKAS LAY ON HIS BED in the village, contemplating the ceiling and inwardly railing against the boredom of waiting. *The Man with the Golden Gun,* retrieved from Gerry's room, lay open at his side, but he couldn't concentrate on the story.

He wished Nadia were here. Oh, the policeman in him knew he'd done the right thing in sending her away, but as a man he wished she were here. She would have made the waiting easier.

He consoled himself with the knowledge that she was safe. Neither Paros nor his henchman Halias could get her.

Then why did he have this uneasy feeling? Was it only the storm, or a sense of impending danger?

After tolling for an hour at dusk, the bell had fallen mercifully silent again. It was nearly over. On Saturday the mourning would be less pronounced as the people shopped and cooked and waited in anticipation of the resurrection celebration.

He could hear the murmur of the patrons in the coffee shop downstairs and thought about joining them. The noisy company would speed the passing of time. And perhaps someone could tell him who the old woman was, and where he could find her. He'd searched the village after Nadia's departure, but she'd apparently vanished off the face of the earth.

Book in hand, he got up and walked to the window, staring out into the lightning-strafed night. The storm was far away. The rain would probably hold off until after midnight, perhaps not come at all.

He tossed the book onto the bed. It fell facedown, pages splayed on the wrinkled blanket. "What the hell?"

Picking up the yellowed clipping that had fluttered free, he stared at it, his eyes widening as he took it in. It was a grainy newspaper photo. One of the four men was a prominent political leader, forty years ago. The man next to him wore a military uniform, colonel's rank. The remaining two—

A cold spasm swept through him. Striding to the door, he pushed his feet into his shoes and headed for the stairs.

Gabriel wasn't in. The dispatcher reminded Lukas in a bored voice that it was after office hours. Lukas tried his home number. No reply. Frustrated, he slammed down the phone, earning himself a severe look from the bartender.

Hitching a hip onto a stool, he sat for a moment with his chin resting on his palm. *Anthea.* She had promised to check into the postwar era for him.

Quickly he dialed his home number. She answered.

"I can't get hold of Gabriel, Mother. I thought you might be able to help me. Did you get any more information on Andreas Paros?"

"Nothing you don't already know. I saw Gabriel yesterday at the law courts. He told me that everything dealing with Gerald Parker is in classified files, so there's no help there, either. It's spooky. Why?"

He briefly considered telling her, but his interpretation of the photo, without any substantiation other than a hunch, might be wrong. The images weren't very clear, and the newsprint had faded and deteriorated with time.

"Just an idea I had." He buried his fingers in his hair, squeezing the muscles at the base of his skull. "We think we've located Paros. I'm waiting for Gabriel's men."

"Good," said Anthea. She paused for an instant, then added in a quiet voice, "What about Nadia? How is it going with her?"

"She's fine."

Anthea tutted. He could just visualize the half amused, half frustrated expression on her face. "I mean you and Nadia. I never doubted that she would be fine with you there. So what's the story?"

No use trying to fool his mother, Lukas knew from past experience. "We've reached an understanding," he said carefully.

Anthea made a sound of disbelief. "If she's to be my daughter-in-law, I'd like to know." Her tone was dry.

Lukas grinned in spite of the worry that gnawed at his gut. "When I convince her, you'll be the first to know."

"When do you think you'll have this wrapped up?"

His smile faded. "Didn't Nadia phone you? She should have by now."

"Why, was she supposed to?" Anthea asked. "I haven't heard from her, and I've been here all evening."

"Damn!" A sudden dread clenched his stomach.

"What was that, dear?"

"Sorry, Mother. I have to go." He hung up.

Nadia hadn't phoned. Had she forgotten? Or—hadn't she reached Ioannina?

He dialed the hotel, getting an answer after twenty rings. The clerk's voice was muffled with sleep. The answer to his terse question confirmed his worst fears.

Nadia never reached Ioannina.

Where was she? With Gerry, assuming he was alive? Had she somehow located him, or had he found her?

Or was she with Paros? If that were the case, he was sure she was in trouble.

He tried Gabriel's home number again, and this time found him there. The information he imparted was complete, and gave Lukas the break he had been waiting for. And he confirmed that reinforcements were on the way.

With a peculiar mixture of elation and renewed fear for Nadia, he reached into his pocket and took out a handful of change, which he tossed onto the bar for the calls. "I'll be back."

Aware of the puzzled stares from the bartender and his customers, he went out into the night.

AN HOUR LATER Lukas was hiking through the canyon that bordered the village, following a well-defined track. He could have driven his car, but since the distance wasn't great and he didn't want to advertise his presence, he'd decided to go on foot.

He shifted the pack on his back, his eyes straining through the darkness. Moonlight illuminated the path fitfully, whenever the heavy clouds shifted, but mostly he had to rely on guesswork and the occasional flares from his flashlight that he allowed himself.

He knew where he was going. Constable Demos hadn't been exactly forthcoming with directions, but a little persuasion and a threat to have him demoted to an even remoter village had loosened his tongue. After initially denying all knowledge of Paros, he had eventually spilled out more information than Lukas needed. Demos had given a description of Paros's house and told him how to reach it.

Lukas wouldn't have minded having him along. He might have to deal with more than just Halias when he found Paros.

He crossed the meadow before the house without incident. Nothing moved. No dogs barked. Only a couple of windows were dimly lighted. He glanced at one on the upper floor. Was Nadia in the house, a prisoner?

He crept around the house, looking for a window that might be unlocked. The tower appeared promising, but the only door he found was of heavy oak and had probably been barred from the inside. The windows, mere slits, were too narrow to admit an adult body.

Reaching the back of the massive building, he paused in the dense shadows of a storage shed. All his senses alert, he listened. Not a sound could be heard, not even the murmur of the doves that might be expected to inhabit the apple trees in the kitchen garden.

He was about to move forward again, to try the rear door, when he froze. Was that a footstep, the crunch of a pebble under a shoe? Tensing, he reached inside his jacket.

Too late.

"I wouldn't, if I were you, Mister Nosy Cop."

With a dismal sinking in his stomach, Lukas felt the cold blade of a knife touch his throat.

Chapter Fourteen

Nadia couldn't sleep. Her body felt lethargic, heavy, especially after the brandy she had consumed on top of the wine at dinner. But her mind raced, conjuring up all sorts of horrifying scenarios.

Even though Paros was obviously planning to leave within the next few days, he wasn't going to leave any witnesses behind. He hadn't evaded the law all these years by being careless.

The only thought that kept her from falling into deep despair was the hope that Paros would let her live long enough for Lukas to come. Lukas had said it would be over by Sunday at the latest. Therefore he must be expecting the reinforcements to storm Paros's hideout before then.

Oh, let him come soon, she prayed desperately. *Oh, Lukas, why didn't I trust you, tell you everything? I wouldn't be in this predicament now.*

She rolled over in the bed, sticking her head under the pillow to shut out the frantic cry of violins. The whole house seemed to be wired for sound, although there was no speaker in the room. But the one in the hall, outside the locked door, was near enough. She was never going to listen to Vivaldi again.

Sometime after midnight, the music stopped. She was drifting on the edge of sleep when a commotion in the hall brought her upright in bed. Heavy footsteps could be heard, then the scrabble of the key in the lock.

The door burst open and Paros came into the room, his hand clutching the scruff of the wolf's neck. In his other hand he held her suitcase. "You might be more comfortable in your nightgown," he said, his cold eyes on the jeans and shirt she hadn't removed.

He stepped aside, calming the wolf as it snarled. "And here is your lover. Enjoy your last night together."

With that, Halias came into view behind him. He threw Lukas's backpack onto the floor, then shoved Lukas into the room after it, nearly pushing him over with the force of his hand on his back.

The two men backed out, and a moment later Nadia heard the lock click with a dreadful finality.

"Oh, Lukas," she cried, tears spilling from her eyes. She launched herself into his arms. He staggered under the force of her embrace, wrapping his arms tightly around her.

"Yeah, I'm glad to see you, too." His smile was ironic. "But this wasn't exactly how I pictured our next meeting."

He put her at arm's length, his smile fading as anger flared in his eyes. "Just how the hell did you get here? You were supposed to be in Ioannina. Why didn't you do as I told you? You realize you've messed everything up."

She gulped, fighting back the flood of tears. Pressing against him, she hid her face against his shirt, grabbing a precarious comfort from the warm, musky scent of him. "Oh, Lukas, it was the old woman. She tried to warn me—no, not just this afternoon—this morning at the cave. But I thought it was about you. It was actually about him."

"You mean Paros. But how did you find this place?"

"There was a map, in Gerry's notebook." She tightened her hand on Lukas's arm. "Lukas, I don't know if he's alive or dead. Paros is capable of anything."

Lukas made a sound of disgust. "The man's mad."

Nadia stiffened. Her fingers uncurled and she slowly pushed herself away, moving over to the window and standing there with her arms around her chest.

"Nadia, what is it?" Coming up behind her, he laid his hands on her shoulders, but she shook them off. She began to pace around the room, agitation in the puppetlike stiffness of her steps.

"Paros is my father," she said, the words ringing with stark clarity in the room. "I'm the daughter of that monster, that madman." She turned, her eyes filling with tears of anguish. "How can you even stand to touch me?"

Lukas reached her in one stride and folded her close, keeping her against him despite her brief struggle to pull free. "Nadia, you don't know if he's telling the truth. Besides, you're not him."

"What if I inherited his...?" Her voice was muffled against his shirt.

"I doubt it," Lukas said, interrupting her. "I doubt if megalomania is hereditary. And in any case, it would have shown up by this time, if you had. I think you're safe."

"What I don't understand is how they managed to hide it from me. Did they lie about my birth date?"

Laughter rumbled in his chest, under her ear. "Don't draw conclusions just yet. You might be related to that bastard, but maybe not as closely as you think." He turned and groped in his pack, coming up with a book she recognized as the novel from Gerry's room. "Look at this."

She stared at the faded picture. "Two of them?"

"And Gabriel confirms that at least until the early fifties Paros had a twin. After that, he's not sure. One of them apparently dropped out of sight." He led her to the bed, where they both sat on the edge of the mattress. Keeping his arm around her, he snuggled her close to his side. "It may be premature to speculate, but this man here might not be your father, or Gerry's, either."

"But he and Gerry and I all have the same eyes. It can't be a coincidence."

"It can be," Lukas stated, "if they were twins."

Nadia sagged against him, weak with relief. But it was a short-lived respite. "If that's true, where is his twin? Just a minute." She reached into her hip pocket and pulled out the photo from Gerry's room. "I suppose this must be Andreas. But the man out there—is he Andreas or his twin?" She stared at the picture, the perfect replica of the man who held them prisoner. "Or are we crazy?"

"Not crazy." Lukas poked a finger at the photo. "See that mole on his right cheek, above the corner of the mouth? Did Paros have it? I don't remember any marks on his face."

Nadia frowned, picturing the man as he'd sat across the table from her. "No, he didn't have a mole." Her face fell. "But he could have had it removed. Many people do. This picture's not very recent, either."

"I suppose," Lukas admitted. "In any case, we can't get away from the conclusion that they were in business together, since there is no recent record of two men named Paros, only of Andreas. When you think of it, it's a perfect setup. While one brother could be making a deal somewhere, the other could be highly visible a thousand miles away. The perfect alibi. It helps explain why they've never been caught."

"Do you think Gerry knew?"

Lukas sighed. "I don't know. If his sources were as good as we think, he probably did. Gabriel found out that Paros was never investigated for war crimes. The islanders apparently forewent making a report of complaint about him with the Allies—probably out of some misguided blood loyalty to a fellow Greek. As far as legal agencies are concerned, he surfaced in the sixties as an arms dealer. The monk's story, of course, ties it all together. And my guess is that your brother also found out."

"Was Gerry an agent, for certain?"

"I've got people still checking that out, Nadia. Remember, it's been only a week since all of this first exploded." Lukas exhaled sharply, and Nadia sensed his frustration. "We'll know sooner if we find Gerald alive."

"If we find him. If he's alive." What Paros had said could be interpreted several ways, she realized. She could only hope. "And where is Andreas or whoever's twin?"

"Good question," Lukas said. "There is no record of his death, at least not as far as Gabriel could ascertain. By the way, the other brother's name was Angelo."

"And which one is that person out there?"

Lukas lifted the curling photo. "Probably Angelo, if this is Andreas. Only fingerprints would prove it, one way or the other. Since both were in the Greek army during the war their prints would be on record."

"Are you sure it was the Greek army?"

His mouth turned up at one corner. "Yes, but I suppose you're thinking with their inclinations they might have been more suited for the Nazi army. No, Nadia, it was only later that they got involved in their present business. Though inklings of their tendencies must've come through when they sent those children from Atalanti."

A little silence fell. Nadia listened to Lukas's quiet breathing, the creaking of the house around them. The window frame rattled as the wind gusted and died. Far away a wolf howled, the lonely wailing making goose bumps rise on her skin. She shuddered as Paros's "pet" answered from somewhere inside the house. "That wolf gives me the willies," she said. "It's as if he can read your thoughts."

"Yeah, I know what you mean. Paros told me if I tried to run, the wolf would attack without mercy."

Nadia gave a shaky laugh. Their situation appeared desperate, but together they might still find a way out.

Lukas hugged her tighter, as if he instinctively knew she needed his reassurance. "I suppose you've checked to see if there's any way out of this room, have you?"

"Hours ago," Nadia confirmed. "There are bars at the windows. From outside they look like flimsy ornamental ironwork, but they're welded into a frame on the walls. And the door hinges can't be removed." She cast a hopeful look at Lukas's backpack. "Unless you've got a sledgehammer in there?"

"No sledgehammer." He let her go and began to prowl around the room, tapping on the walls, especially in the bathroom, which had probably been converted from a dressing room. All the walls were solid granite, he guessed about a meter thick. No way out at all. The door was as Nadia had said, constructed of thick oak planks and installed with hinges that would resist any attempt to remove them, short of an assault with a blowtorch. It did however have a heavy brass bolt on the inside, which he threw closed. They might not be able to leave the room, but neither Paros nor Halias would be able to get in.

Not that that would stop them from killing Nadia and himself. All the signs pointed to Paros's imminent departure. They had only to set the place on fire when they left. Despite the stone walls, a fire in the hall outside would engulf Lukas and Nadia in short order.

Besides, he was sure that Paros, being in the arms business, would be able to scare up a mortar, or a machine gun armed with bullets that could easily penetrate the door and slice them to ribbons.

The window would have been ideal as an escape route. It was only ten feet above the ground, and the open meadow lay beyond it. While the grass would not provide much cover, they could probably make it to the mountain gorge in the dark. From there it wasn't far to the village.

However, the curlicues over the glass were made of wrought iron, the spaces between them much too small for even a child to pass through.

He gazed speculatively at the light fixture. Nadia followed his glance. "If you were MacGyver, you'd rig something to electrocute Halias when he comes in the door."

"Who the hell's MacGyver?"

"It's a television series. The hero's always getting out of tight situations by using material around him."

"Well, to do that, we'd have to have materials around us," Lukas said sardonically. "They took away anything I could use as a tool or a weapon. Besides, fooling around with two hundred twenty volts, you're more likely to electrocute yourself than your enemy. Nadia, I hate to say this, but it doesn't look good."

"So we have to count on a lucky break tomorrow," Nadia said, fatigue and despair giving her voice the fragility of a thread.

"Let's sleep on it," Lukas said. In about twenty-four hours there would be more cops around here than Paros or Halias could handle, he thought. But he was seriously beginning to wonder if they would be alive to see it. "We're both tired. Maybe in the morning we'll see a way to get out of here. They'll have to feed us, for one. That means they'll open the door."

"Why should they feed us if they're going to kill us?" Tears stung her eyes. It couldn't end like this.

"Because they haven't killed us yet. That means they've got some plan about how they're going to do it. As long as we're alive, we have a chance." He paused, his eyes burning into hers as if he wanted to transfer some of his indomitable will to her. "If we keep our wits about us."

He stood up, pulling off his jacket and unbuttoning his shirt. "I'd like to take a shower. You don't mind, do you?"

"Mind? Why should I mind?" Nadia's voice trembled and again she was close to tears. She rubbed at her eyes angrily. *Funny.* She hadn't felt like crying all the time Paros was looming over her. Now that Lukas was here, she couldn't seem to control the urge to weep.

Bare-chested, his jeans hanging low on his hips, he sauntered into the bathroom and turned on the shower. "Come with me, Nadia. The water's hot. It'll warm you."

She had showered earlier, but the sight of Lukas's broad chest with the dark mat of curls made her change her mind.

Pushing aside all thoughts of danger, she stepped into the bathroom, which was steaming like a sauna. Lukas closed the door behind them.

He began to get undressed—and stopped. "That's another thing. I don't think this guy is your father. What father would encourage his daughter to spend a last night with her lover?"

"The kind of father who kills people, or gives others the means to do so and calls it business," Nadia said tightly. "Besides, it's not as if he brought me up, or could feel any sense of responsibility toward me." Sally's words came back to ring in her ears. "He didn't care for Sally. He only wanted to dominate her."

Lukas stared at her. "Do you trust me, Nadia?"

She came forward until her bare toes touched his. She ignored the cold that seeped up from the stone floor. The air was warm from the running shower. Leaning toward him, she placed her lips lightly on his. "Yes, Lukas." Her breath sweetly caressed his face. "Yes, Lukas, I trust you. With everything."

They washed each other, the soap making their skin slippery, endangering their footing on the tiles. Nadia was shy at first but Lukas's open pleasure in her touch soon overcame her remaining inhibitions.

"I want to kiss you," she whispered recklessly, drunk with the feel of him, the sensuality.

Lukas felt a jolt like lightning in his body. He wanted to hold her, keep her, protect her, and for a moment he shook with helpless rage at his inability to do so. But then she circled his waist with her arms—and he thought no more.

THEY SLEPT DEEPLY, wrapped around each other under the dusty woolen blankets. At dawn, when the sky was an angry red among the massed storm clouds, they made love again, slowly and gently, with a quiet desperation that had both of them fighting tears afterward.

"If I've got you pregnant, we're in serious trouble," Lukas said as they were dressing later.

"If they kill us, it hardly makes a difference." Again Nadia felt tears sting in her eyes, her sadness encompassing the future she and Lukas might never have.

Odd how quickly things changed. A couple of days ago she was thinking of the futility of loving him. Now with a finite future, none of the difficulties and differences in background seemed to matter.

If they got out of this alive, they could work out the rest.

As if he read her thoughts, Lukas came over and tilted her chin up with his fingers. "Don't give up yet, Nadia. If there's a way out of this, we'll find it. And then we'll work on the future. Promise me one thing. If we make it, will you marry me?"

Pain squeezed her heart. She closed her eyes, as if by shutting out the room she could deny the reality of their danger. "Yes, Lukas, I'll marry you." The words were torn out of her, and she could not control the tears that flowed over her cheeks. Lukas held her and wished he could indulge in the same release she surrendered to.

But he could not afford the luxury.

Not yet.

THE DAY PASSED in endless tedium. A surly Kyriakos Halias brought them breakfast, leaving the tray without a word, and locking the door securely after him. If he heard the drawing of the bolt on the prisoners' side of the door, he didn't consider it worthy of comment.

After Nadia and Lukas had eaten the sparse meal of bread and strong black coffee, they waited for Halias's return.

"If this is our last meal," Nadia joked in a feeble attempt to relieve their tension, "it certainly isn't much."

The distinct chop-chop of helicopter blades passing close over the house stifled Lukas's reply. They both rushed to the window.

A large cargo helicopter painted in camouflage colors settled down onto the meadow. The grass undulated in waves until the rotors stopped turning. Several men climbed out of the machine, walking over to meet a Land Rover that was coming into view from the direction of the house. They climbed inside, and the vehicle made a wide turn before coming back.

Throughout the morning the men made numerous trips with the Land Rover, loading furniture and crates into the chopper. Even through the closed window, Nadia and Lukas could hear Halias shouting orders, directing the work. Paros came out a couple of times, dressed in a dark suit and holding his wolf on a leash, but he left the supervision up to his burly associate.

The helicopter lifted off before noon into a lowering charcoal sky. It was back soon after the captives had consumed their lunch of lukewarm lentil soup. Halias had taken the breakfast tray when he brought the lunch, but they had had no opportunity to jump him. A cold-eyed man they hadn't seen before, standing outside their door armed with an Uzi, stopped short any show of heroics.

"They can't be going far," Nadia said as the helicopter landed for the second time.

"They probably have a ship docked somewhere near Igoumenitsa," Lukas suggested. He glared at the locked door. "Damn it, if they're going to keep us here, they could at least let us have a little peace."

"Be glad there's no speaker in this room," Nadia said, hunching her shoulders more securely into the blanket she had wrapped around herself. Although the water in the bath was still warm, Paros must have turned off the central heating system. The radiator under the window had been cold since Nadia had been shut up in the room after dinner last night. At first residual warmth had kept the room reasonably comfortable, but now it was decidedly chilly.

"If there was," Lukas said grimly, "I'd have torn it out. I'm beginning to dislike Vivaldi intensely."

Vivaldi wasn't the only composer Paros played. For some hours they'd been forced to listen to ponderous tones and operatic shrieks that Nadia was sure was Wagner. Now they were being treated to a frenetic violin chorus celebrating autumn.

Nadia lay on the bed, pulling the blanket around her ears. If only the waiting would end. She was beginning to understand how prisoners on death row must feel, year after year of postponements. At the end, their execution must be a relief.

She and Lukas had talked about their childhoods, education, work. But the future was left out. What was the use of discussing a future when you weren't sure you'd have one?

She knew she loved him, profoundly. The complexity of him, the sensitivity with which he treated her and the tender light in his wonderful eyes when he glanced at her made him a man who was unique. A man who wasn't ashamed to show his love.

However briefly their lives had intertwined, she had been changed, enriched by their association.

THE HELICOPTER LEFT for the second time near sunset, heightening the tension that gripped them. Each time they heard a sound in the house, their eyes met, Nadia's fearful, Lukas's reassuring, as warm as the clasp of his fingers around hers.

She envied his serenity, his ability to wait patiently, his lack of anxiety in the face of death. Only by whipping up anger at the arrogance of the man keeping them prisoner could she hold her terror at bay.

"It's not fair," she blurted out. "It's just not fair."

Lukas smiled, his eyes tranquil as the sea at dawn. He had removed his bandage, and all that remained of his wound was a thin dark scar edged with pink new skin. He squeezed her hand. "Don't worry, Nadia. There's always a chance."

They knew Halias and Paros were still in the house. The two of them had returned in the Land Rover after they'd seen off the chopper. But since then silence had fallen. Even the music had stopped shortly after dark.

Two of them. And the wolf. Nadia turned over various plans in her mind. Lukas was a professional. If she could create a distraction long enough for him to overpower one of the men and get hold of a gun, they might have a chance.

"How far is it to the village?" she asked.

Lukas regarded her questioningly before he answered. "Four or five kilometers. Why?"

"And your car, where is it?" She groped in her jeans pocket. "I still have the extra keys you gave me."

"It's in the village. I hiked here and got caught outside. But Nadia, I don't think it's going to work. First we'd have to get out of this room, and we know that's impossible. Secondly, they've probably moved the car." His mouth hardened into a thin line. "But I'll tell you one thing. We're not going to just sit and let them shoot us like ducks at a fair. If I see a chance I'll jump them."

"And I'll help you,' Nadia promised, squelching down a quiver of fear. Could she, if it came down to it, kill a man?

They lay on the bed, fully dressed, wrapped in the blankets. As the evening advanced, cold seeped into every corner of the room, until their breath condensed like smoke in the air. For a while they napped, but the anxious waiting kept them in a state of jumpy tension.

When would Paros come?

Nadia started out of a fitful doze. The overhead light still burned, indicating that the power was on. She glanced at her watch. Eleven o'clock. She wondered if the radio equipment had been moved, or if it remained in the den.

Lukas was awake as well, his head raised in an attitude of listening. Outside the wind had picked up, banging a shutter nearby. Thunder rumbled ominously in the distance.

The steady beat of footsteps sounded in the hall. Two sets.

A key grated in the lock and the door flew open. Lukas had not reset the bolt since their last meal. Since they couldn't escape from the room, there was no use shutting out their captors.

Paros, with his pet at his side regarding them with hungrily gleaming eyes, stood framed by the doorway. Halias stood in the background, his hard face set in watchfulness, the barrel of his rifle never wavering from its targets. "Come. It's time," Paros said.

And he laughed, a maniacal peal that reverberated up and down the stone corridor.

Chapter Fifteen

The laughter died into eerie echoes. Paros watched them closely for a long moment, his eyes glittering as he gauged their reactions.

"By the way, Mr. Stylianos," he said at last in the placid tone of a man discussing the weather, "you might be interested to know that the men you sent for have been delayed." He made a clicking sound with his tongue. "An unfortunate rock slide has blocked the road. It may take several days to clear."

Nadia looked at Lukas, masking the dismay in her heart. That meant they couldn't drive out, either, even if they could reach the car.

"An unfortunate slide?" Lukas asked, his brows lifting. "Or simply an expedient one? It doesn't take much to start a slide at this time of year. And what about you? How are you driving out of here?"

Paros gave a low chuckle that sent an icy shiver over Nadia's skin. "Tomorrow the helicopter will be back. I don't need the road."

"And you think a slide will stop my men?" Lukas asked, his eyes shifting restlessly as he searched for a sign of weakness, an opening. But when he experimentally stepped closer to Paros, the wolf lunged with dripping fangs bared, nearly breaking his master's grip.

"Not stop them," Paros said. Nadia for the first time noticed he was garbed in a navy, pin-striped suit, looking as if he would be more at home in a board meeting than in a mountain stronghold, planning a double murder. "Merely delay them. By noon tomorrow I'll be gone from here."

"Then why kill us?" It went against the grain for Lukas to press, but he had to try, for Nadia's sake. He had taken up his career with a clear knowledge of its inherent dangers. He had always known the day would come when he wouldn't be able to talk, bargain or fight his way out of a tight situation. Nadia's involvement, on the other hand, had come not from choice but from concern for her brother. She didn't deserve this.

"I've been successful, mainly because I don't make mistakes," Paros said complacently. "Or leave behind witnesses."

Lukas leaped to the attack. "Did you do that to Gerald Parker? Kill him?"

Again the maniacal laughter sounded in the room. Paros glanced at Halias as if weighing his thoughts. Deciding, he turned back to Nadia and Lukas. "Don't you know? He's still alive. He escaped, because my dear brother let sentiment override necessity."

"Escape?" Nadia blurted. "Is he alive?"

"Yes, he's alive—for now." The man's tone was bitter.

Elation filled Nadia despite the harshly uttered words. Gerry was alive! Suddenly another question came to mind. "Which Paros are you, Andreas or Angelo?"

Paros frowned, his eyes blazing now with the cold fire of sapphires. "I see Mr. Stylianos has been babbling." He looked at Lukas. "I was afraid you would find out. The village operator told me about your calls to Athens."

"Well, which one are you?" Clenching her hands into fists, Nadia moved forward, stopping only when the wolf growled.

"I'm Angelo." His smile was thin, evil. "It pleased me to tell you I was your father." His accent was suddenly more pronounced and he exhaled slowly, the only sign that he might be capable of emotion. "He didn't want me to kill Gerald. He tried to stop me. In the scuffle Gerald was wounded, but managed to flee. Andreas was killed."

"And you buried him in the grave marked with Gerald's headstone," Lukas put in. His last conversation with Constable Demos had revealed that the village policeman hadn't even examined the body. Gerry's men had reported the death, brought in the personal effects, and hastened the burial in a closed coffin. Demos couldn't clean his hands of the mess soon enough.

"Yes." Angelo's eyes were empty, like deep volcanic lakes. "It was a simple matter to place his body in the empty coffin that was supposed to contain Parker. They resembled one another, you see, and everyone was only too happy to close the case. I'll miss him, even though he sometimes didn't have the stomach for our business." His voice hardened, taking on an edge that promised violence. "After all, he married that little fool Sally. Well, I got rid of her."

More pieces of the puzzle fell into place. "So that's how Sally managed to get away from him," Nadia said. "You gave her a chance to escape. And you kept him from going after her all these years. Did she know there were two of you?"

Paros laughed again, a wheezing cackle this time that went on as if he couldn't stop, until tears ran down his face. Nadia wanted to clap her hands over her ears to shut out the demented sounds. Finally it subsided into a hacking cough, forcing him to take out a handkerchief to wipe his eyes. "She never knew. I found it amusing."

Nadia shrank back in horror.

"The few times I came to the village when Andreas wasn't around, I gave her a hard time. She always threw me out of the house. A spirited woman, I'll give you that."

For a moment Paros looked thoughtful. Then he smiled craftily. "Come, it's high time we were moving, if we're to reach the village by midnight."

He stepped back and Halias gestured with the rifle for them to walk ahead.

THE TWIN BEAMS from the Land Rover's headlights provided the only steady illumination in the windy night. The moon had risen but it played hide-and-seek with the clouds. At intervals the surrounding mountain peaks were silhouetted by lightning that lit up the countryside in flashes.

Paros drove the Rover with Lukas seated beside him. In the back seat Halias held the rifle muzzle pressed to Nadia's ribs. Paros had nodded his satisfaction at the arrangement, fixing his eyes on Lukas. "You won't endanger her life, will you, Mr. Stylianos?" he had said in a voice that rasped like torn silk. "One move and she'll die in the most painful manner, shot in the stomach. I'm sure you wouldn't want that."

So Lukas had sat helpless, grinding his teeth and making wild and futile plans, none of them remotely workable.

The moment they entered the village, Lukas realized that the electricity was off. The street lamps and houses were enveloped in darkness. Keeping his expression neutral, he turned over various possibilities in his mind. Would the darkness work against them, or could they make use of it?

None of the villagers would be likely to help them, that was certain. Lukas already knew from the unfriendly reception he'd endured from everyone including Constable Demos that blood loyalty would bind the local people to Paros.

Although he didn't think they would condone cold-blooded murder, they would turn a blind eye to any activity short of that.

The streets were deserted, the houses shuttered. The entire population appeared to have crowded into the square, which was lit by torches lashed to poles. On a platform near the church door two priests chanted, words snatched by the wind.

Lukas wondered what Nadia must be thinking of the ritual. Although he'd witnessed the Easter celebration many times, and understood its deep spiritual significance, to Nadia it must appear as alien as a druid sacrifice.

"Unfortunately the slide knocked out the power and telephone wires," Paros informed them.

That meant they were strictly on their own, Lukas realized. No way to call for help, even if he could reach a telephone.

"There have been an inordinate number of 'accidents' here lately," he said conversationally. "Were you responsible for the damage to the machinery at the quarry?"

Paros dipped his head, his smile complacent. "I thought when Gerald's body was found they would blame the death on an angry worker getting even for the damage. Gerald never came near the machinery. It was Kyriakos."

"Clever, aren't you?" Lukas said sardonically.

He turned his head and glanced at Nadia as the Land Rover stopped behind his own parked car. In the fitful light her face was pale, her hair loosened from its braid by the wind. She looked composed, as if resigned to her fate, but the knotted muscle at the edge of her jaw told him she shared his determination not to give up until the very end.

"We are going to mix with the crowd," Paros said. "I want your deaths to look like a simple accident, in case I have to return to Greece at some time in the future. I don't want the specter of a murder investigation hanging over my head."

"What about Gerald?" Lukas asked.

"No one can prove anything. Kyriakos will take care of him, or one of my allies in the village. These simple shepherds will do almost anything for the right price. It will also look like an accident, a man falling over a cliff, or a car going off the road into a deep ravine. Once he's found. And believe me, he will be. My retinue is large."

He pulled a tiny pistol from his inside suit pocket, prodding Lukas with it. "We will all mingle with the crowd, make sure people see us. Then they will see you get into your car and drive away. When you go off the road at the bridge, the case will be quickly closed. A regrettable incident, but these roads are known to be treacherous." He glanced at the sky. At intervals sheets of lightning turned the night into a lurid day. "Especially during a storm."

Lukas's mind raced as he stepped out of the Land Rover. He kept his head down, feigning defeat. In reality he could see the flaws in Paros's plan, flaws that he might be able to turn to Nadia's and his advantage.

Paros kept the pistol pressed into his back as they joined the crowd. Lukas glanced at his watch. Almost midnight. He placed an arm around Nadia's waist. Her rigidity relaxed slightly but he knew she braced herself against the possibility that Halias might grow impatient and pull the trigger on the rifle at her side.

This could be the moment they'd been waiting for.

LIGHTNING FLARED, and Lukas trod on the toe of the man next to him.

The man let out an indignant yelp and shifted sharply, bumping against Paros. The instant he felt the pressure of the gun leave him, Lukas jerked Nadia away, managing to put the bodies of two or three burly villagers between them and their killers. The ranks closed again, and he heard Paros and Halias swearing, then being told to shut up by an irate shepherd.

Lukas had to increase the distance, but the congregation stood packed around them. Paros couldn't get to them, but neither could they escape the crowd.

The chanting approached a crescendo. Beneath his breath he echoed the familiar litany. He knew the high point of the mass was almost upon them. At any moment the priests' assistants would be dousing the torches, if the wind didn't do it for them.

Yes. One blew out as the wind gusted, and the others were grabbed by nearby men and extinguished in buckets of water. The darkness was complete, and except for the rising savagery of the storm there was silence.

"Now, Nadia!" Lukas yelled under cover of a deafening roar of thunder. Streaks of lightning flashed almost continuously across the sky.

Gripping her hand securely in his, he ducked his head and charged through the packed worshippers. Their attention was fixed on the priest who was about to light the first candle that symbolized the resurrection, and they parted to let the couple through.

"Quick, before they get clear and start shooting." Nadia felt the muscles in her legs stretch as she ran to keep up with Lukas. Static electricity snapped around them, setting their hair on end.

Behind them the triumphant chant rose into the black, stormy sky. *Christós anesti.* Christ is risen. Now firecrackers and gunshots competed with the thunder for noise, and Nadia braced herself in case one of the shots was aimed at them.

"The keys," Lukas panted as they reached the dubious shelter of the car. "Do you have them?"

She'd clutched them in her hand since they'd joined the Easter crowd. "Here." She thrust them toward him.

It took him far less time to open the door than it had taken her the other night. In a moment they were in the car. Lukas pushed in the ignition key, praying Paros hadn't tampered with the electrical system.

The engine turned over at once. A glance in the rearview mirror told him Paros and Halias were just fighting their way free of the crowd. The candles the people held flicked on one by one, a multitude of fireflies in competition with the storm.

Lukas gunned the engine, roaring out of the square with the headlights off, navigating mainly by memory, with a little help from the erratic flashes of lightning.

"The house!" Nadia shouted, closing her eyes as a brick wall materialized out of the gloom in front of them. Lukas dragged the wheel around, then took a quick turn onto another street that was little more than a goat track. A fender scraped against a stone wall, rocking the little car on its wheels. "We have to go back to Paros's house."

Lukas fought with the steering wheel as the car sped down the road. "Are you crazy? After all the trouble we've had to get away from there?"

"You heard what he said about the road. They've got us trapped. The last place they'll expect us to go is back to the house. From there you can call for help."

"The lines are down." He careened around another corner, looking for a road, any road that would lead out of the village and into the mountains, where they could hide.

"Paros has a radiotelephone," Nadia said.

He slammed on the brakes. "A radiotelephone? Are you sure?"

"Yes, I'm sure. It was in his den."

Lukas stamped down on the clutch and shoved the car back into gear. It took off like a scalded rabbit. "Why didn't you tell me this before? I was beginning to think we'd be forced to let the bastard get away. I'll call the Ioannina police station and get them to send the men in by helicopter."

On reaching the house, they discovered that the front door was locked, but they soon found the back door had an easier latch to breach. With a special burglar's tool Lukas always carried in his car, he swung the door open.

"Quite a talent you've got there," Nadia commented dryly.

He tossed her a grin, his eyes gleaming recklessly. "Thanks. It's come in handy a few times."

THE MAN LAY in the grass at the far side of the meadow, his night vision binoculars trained on the house. He watched as the Renault pulled up in front of the door, its yellow paint glowing under the lamp.

Expecting pursuit, he waited. Time passed, perhaps ten minutes.

He decided it was enough. Getting up from his prone position, he winced as he flexed his left arm. The damp night air had stiffened the barely healed wound and a dull ache pulsed there—more of an annoyance than a disability.

He was about to head across the field when Paros's Land Rover, headlights blazing, roared down the rough track. He sank back into the grass, raising the binoculars once more.

The two men, accompanied by the wolf, leaped out and ran into the tower door, leaving it ajar.

The silent watcher rose to his feet, and started across the meadow in a smooth catlike lope.

THE ELECTRONIC EQUIPMENT was still in the study, although all the books and most of the furniture had been removed. Lukas sat down in front of it and punched out a series of numbers. "Damn."

"What's wrong?" Nadia asked. "Don't you know how to work it?"

"Yeah, I know how to work it, but it's hooked up to the computer. It needs an access code. Do you know anything about computers?"

"I know something," Nadia allowed, frowning as she studied the blinking cursor on the monitor. "But if we don't know the code—"

"It has to be something to do with the man himself," Lukas said, clenching and unclenching his fists impatiently. "Let me think—what did Gabriel say about him?"

"His nickname!" Nadia exclaimed. She typed in "*Lýkos*" on the keyboard, her fingers sure and accurate.

Nothing. The cursor blinked smugly.

"Damn, it doesn't work."

"It doesn't?" Lukas thought for an instant. "Try again, but this time type an *Ó* and a space before the name. In Greek you always use an article, even with proper names."

Nothing. Nadia tapped her fingers on the desk, her mind racing. "What about 'wolf'?"

That didn't work, either. Nadia felt the muscles at the back of her neck tighten. If they didn't find the code word soon, they'd have to come up with another plan quickly. Time was running out.

Just on the off chance, she typed, "A wolf."

As if by magic, words materialized, spreading like intelligent green bugs over the screen. At the same time an alarm began to clamor through the speaker system all over the house. And worst of all, Vivaldi's violins began their maddening serenade.

"Oh, oh," Lukas muttered. "I thought it strange that there was no alarm, but out here, who would come if it went off? Can you shut if off?"

Nadia gave him a withering look. "What do you think I am, a computer genius? I only know word and data processing. Just make your call."

Despite the shrilling of the alarm, the phone worked. Lukas made the call, fortuitously getting a clear line at once. Flipping off the machine, he turned to Nadia. "They should be here within the hour."

The alarm suddenly fell silent. Both Lukas and Nadia froze. Did it have a time limit? Or had someone shut it off?

"Let's beat it." Lukas grabbed her arm. "I think we've got company."

As they opened the door of the den they heard Paros inside the front entrance shouting orders to Halias. "Guard that hall. I'll get the den. Keep your eye on their car."

The house was large and rambling but with barred or shuttered windows and few exit doors. Lukas and Nadia slipped out of the den in advance of Paros, hearing only his roar of fury as he discovered they'd used the phone despite his precautions. Running down a hall chosen at random, they finally came to a door that was neither locked nor guarded. A narrow stone passage and a steep stairway lay beyond it.

Lukas didn't like the appearance of what could be a dead end. He turned, willing to risk one of the closed rooms they'd passed rather than climb the stairs. But he stopped short when he heard Halias's voice raised in anger as he argued with his boss. At the same time, he either heard or imagined the scrabble of the wolf's claws on the bare stone floor, the panting of an animal's breath as it hunted down some quarry. He wasn't about to wait around to find out if he was hearing aright. If they didn't move now, they'd be cornered.

Dragging Nadia with him, he leaped into the passageway, closing the door behind him. There was no lock or bolt, so he found a pebble on the floor and wedged it under the solid wood. It wasn't much, but it might buy them a little time.

If only he had his gun. He might have narrowed the odds by at least eliminating the wolf.

The door at the top of the stairs let them out onto the flat roof of the tower. There was no way to secure it, but Lukas realized that nothing short of bulletproof steel would stop a determined Paros. Besides, there were probably other ways up.

What concerned him more immediately was finding a way for Nadia and himself to get down. Fast.

The wind howled around them. Nadia staggered under its force as it tore at her clothes and hair. Lukas's black curls tumbled over his forehead. He held tightly to her arm as they circled the roof.

A bolt of flame from the storm overhead lighted the sky with a blinding flare, revealing an escape route that would have been perfect.

Except for the guns that were pointed straight at their chests.

ON SILENT FEET the blond man sped down the dim corridors, following the sound of Paros's orders to Halias. "You fool, if they reach the roof, they'll get away."

The blond man smiled grimly and increased his pace. The door under the staircase stood half open. Could he catch them in time? If the elevator was at the top—if Nadia had used it—

He shook his head. Nadia and her friend wouldn't have known of its existence. He heard the growl of the wolf, Paros's low voice soothing it, and flattened himself against the wall outside the door.

The swish of the elevator reached his ears. *Damn.* Gun cocked, he kicked the door wide.

Too late.

A closed steel grid faced him, and he heard the creaking of the cables as the elevator carried Paros and Halias to the roof.

With a resigned grunt, the man returned to the staircase and began the long run up to the top.

NADIA GROANED. "How did they get up here so fast?"

"An elevator." Paros had to shout above the crash of thunder that reverberated all around them. He and Halias came closer, the guns steady in their hands. The wolf at Paros's side strained to escape the choke chain around its neck.

Beside Nadia, Lukas cursed fluently.

"Neatly trapped," Paros added. "I would have thought better of you, Mr. Stylianos, the crack investigator." His voice softened, carrying faintly over the whine of the wind. "I'm sorry it has to be like this, but it looks as if I'll have to shoot you, after all."

He lifted the gun, sighting down the barrel in a way that guaranteed he wouldn't miss. Nadia watched, her mind detached from her emotions. The gun looked like a toy. Surely it couldn't kill them.

The wind died for an instant, and in the sudden silence the growl of the wolf took on an additional ferocity. The creature with its staring eyes and bared teeth might have been one of the hounds of hell, barely under the control of the man who held it.

Heedless of her own safety, Nadia threw herself toward Paros. She had made it halfway across the roof when Paros released the wolf. Afterward she wasn't sure if he'd done it on purpose or whether he'd been unable to hold the creature.

The animal, enraged and terrified by the storm and whatever signal he was getting from his master, leaped forward.

Nadia, swerving to avoid the powerful body flying through the air toward her, slipped and stumbled, crashing headlong to the concrete.

"Nadia, cover your face." Dimly she heard Lukas's desperate shout but she couldn't move, mesmerized by the salivating jaws of the beast. One of the heavy paws rested on her chest, a weight that made her breath rasp in her throat.

As if from a great distance she heard a whimper and belatedly recognized it as her own voice. The animal's breath, hot and fetid, fanned her face. Closing her eyes, she braced herself for the first tearing attack of the glistening fangs.

It never came. A sharp crack, and the wolf leaped into the air as if jerked by a puppet string. It fell beside her with a heavy thud, the pale eyes glazing.

Paros screamed, whether in rage or remorse at the death of his pet, she couldn't tell. She struggled to her feet, her body racked with shudders.

The sight that met her eyes hit her like a blow to the stomach. She swayed, saving herself by clutching the rail that encircled the roof.

A tall blond man stood at the stair doorway, a gun in his hand.

Gerald. Her mouth formed the word, but no sound came out. Tears ran down her cheeks, expressing both relief and renewed fear. Paros still held a gun, but his expression was less certain, and he seemed confused.

"Gerald!" Nadia cried.

His eyes flicked momentarily to her. "Hi, Nadia. Fancy meeting you here." He grinned slightly before turning to Lukas. "Here, catch."

Lukas neatly fielded the pistol Gerald tossed to him. Flipping off the safety, he pointed it at Halias, who had dropped his rifle, evidently deciding the game was up.

Paros abruptly came back to life, the temporarily stunned look fading. In spite of the guns aimed at him, he made a last attempt to escape.

From the roof a footbridge carved out of solid rock led to the nearby mountain crag. With an extraordinary speed born of desperation, he crossed the span and began to clamber up the slope.

Lukas stuffed the pistol into his belt and grabbed the rifle Halias had dropped. Lifting it to his shoulder, he yelled at Paros. "You've got no chance. Come back."

Paros turned, his face contorted with hatred. He fired the pistol he'd managed to retain throughout the wolf's attack, sending a bullet screaming past their heads.

A crack from Gerald's gun sounded above the storm. He'd hit the rock face below Paros, the spray of shards visible as another streak of lightning flashed. Paros screamed, a shriek of terror so horrible Nadia shuddered.

As if in slow motion the crest of the rock on which Paros stood disintegrated, sliding with deadly precision into the gorge below, taking the end of the bridge with it. Paros vanished in a cloud of dust and debris. All was silent but for the subdued cry of the wind and a rumble of thunder.

Nadia was the first to move. Running across the roof she threw her arms around Gerald. He dropped his gun and hugged her close. "You're all right. You're all right," she whispered over and over.

"Yeah, I'm all right. The reports of my death were greatly exaggerated." She felt him shift his weight and draw in a sharp breath as he looked over her head at

Lukas. "You must be the policeman who's been the talk of the village for two days."

"Yes, I'm Lukas Stylianos."

Gerry let go of Nadia long enough to extend his hand to Lukas. It was then she noticed that his left arm hung limply at his side. "Are you hurt?"

Gerry smiled at her affectionately as he further ruffled the disorder of her hair. "It's not important. I'll live."

Lukas, too, was smiling, although he tried to glare at Nadia. "Dumb move, Nadia, jumping like that. I ought to shoot you for the scare you gave me with that little stunt. But since it turned out okay, I guess I'll let you live."

Herding Halias ahead of them, they went down to the ground floor in the elevator. With both the Renault and the Land Rover at their disposal they transported their prisoner back to the village without a hitch. There the constable scowled in obvious unhappiness, but locked him into the single jail cell.

The lights were still out, but the streets were lively with celebration as the villagers walked home from the church with their candles. Keeping the candles lighted in the wind was no easy matter, but most arrived with their flames intact, shielded by work-worn hands.

On the villagers' faces was a simple joy that moved Nadia deeply. The sorrow of the past week was over; a new day had dawned.

Chapter Sixteen

"But where were you all this time?" Nadia couldn't contain her questions as they sat together in Gerald's room above the coffee shop. At intervals they heard the crack of guns going off, and the whine and pop of exploding firecrackers. Easter celebrations were a noisy affair, in contrast to the funereal silence of Holy Week.

"Why didn't you contact us? You knew how worried we'd be." Her voice rose, anger setting in now that they were all safe. "And the autopsy report—didn't it occur to you that I'd see it and that it wouldn't exactly be nice light reading?"

Gerald swallowed, his blue eyes filling with regret. "Damn it, Nadia. I was sure they'd refuse to let you see it."

"They tried," Nadia said in a wobbly voice. "But I insisted."

"I'm sorry, Nadia. But it had to look real." He shifted on the chair, his demeanor that of an unwilling witness at a trial. "You see, Paros wasn't wanted in Greece. As long as he kept his nose clean, he could live here with impunity. I needed to figure out a way to get a charge laid against him here, or to get him out of the country into a jurisdiction where there was already a warrant for his arrest."

Nadia shuddered. "So he tried to kill you, to save his own skin."

"I got too close," he said simply, as if danger were an element he lived with every day and counted only as a minor inconvenience. "We used the attack to our advantage."

"How?" Lukas spoke for the first time since they'd dropped off Halias. He stood next to the door, arms crossed over his chest as he leaned against the wall.

Gerald looked uncomfortable. "There's a lot of this I'm not supposed to tell."

"I understand." Lukas nodded. "The department—and my mother, who has a few sources of her own—ran into a blank wall of classified files when they tried to get into your background."

"Precautions," Gerald said.

"But you wrote Sally and told her you were going to Atalanti," Nadia interjected.

"Not Sally. The letter was addressed to you. It was a little extra insurance, to give you a place to start looking if something happened. I didn't want to involve you, but I felt I had no choice. My office wasn't able to offer me any backup in this case. If I disappeared or was killed, I knew I could count on you to make sure there was a thorough investigation." He frowned. "How did Sally get the letter?"

"Since I didn't know how long I'd be gone, I had my mail rerouted to their house," Nadia said. "Since it was from you, she must have decided to open it. She told me about it over the phone. She was in an awful panic."

Gerry gaped. "Sally in a panic? That must have been a first. Still, I'm not surprised. It must have seemed like a crazy thing to do, to look up a father I'd no reason to remember with affection."

Disquieting thoughts tumbled over one another in Nadia's mind. She'd thought it a shock to learn the identity of her own father, but to face the reality of Gerry's covert and highly dangerous work would take even more getting used to.

"I checked back and Mother had to have been pregnant with you when she left Greece."

A measure of irony filled Nadia. Andreas might not have been an exemplary human being, but at least he had escaped the depth of perversion that marked Angelo. "I still can't believe that Sally could have kept the secret of my parentage for so many years."

Now Nadia knew the reason behind Sally's uncharacteristic hysteria. She'd known Nadia would discover the secret she'd kept hidden for thirty years. Why had she done that? Probably to spare Nadia the knowledge that her father was a criminal—to spare her the burden that Gerry had carried all his life.

Gerry reached over and squeezed Nadia's hand. "Don't sweat over it, Nadia. She must have thought it best. After all, who did it hurt? And you didn't have to carry the memory of your father's cruelty with you throughout your childhood."

"Maybe I should be glad I never knew him," she said fiercely. Her eyes filled with tears. So many people had been hurt—the children taken from their homes—the victims of the wars Paros had tacitly encouraged. Sally. Gerry. "Was it very bad, Gerry, the first years?"

He shrugged. "Sometimes it was. But after we left him, I did my best to block out that part of my life. Paul Roberts was my father in every way that counted, even though we weren't emotionally close." He drew a deep breath, exhaling slowly. "Anyway, it's all in the past. I came to terms with it a long time ago. That's not why I went after him."

"Andreas Paros, or Angelo, as we now know, has been one of the most elusive criminals of the century," Lukas said. "How did you get into this? Wouldn't your organization have been more likely to send someone who was not personally involved?"

"They would have, but I overrode their objections. As his son—at the time we thought it was Andreas Paros we were dealing with—I had an advantage. And it had to be handled discreetly, with no international incident that would get into the press. Beyond the business of handling my supposed funeral, I was strictly on my own."

"Was it so important you'd take such risks?" Nadia asked.

"Yes." A shadow crossed Gerald's face. "Angelo killed someone I loved dearly. And the baby she was expecting. My child." He rubbed a hand across his eyes, pinching his nose briefly as he fought for control. "Oh, he didn't pull the trigger, and the shot wasn't meant for her. It was meant for me. He knew I'd seen him at an arms dealers' conference in Geneva last year."

He looked at his sister. "Yes, Nadia, there are legitimate weapons dealers, business like anything else.

Angelo knew I'd recognized him and known him for what he was. And he recognized me. You see, they'd kept tabs on me all these years, thanks to Andreas's possessiveness, but he'd never been able to act on his knowledge. Of course at the conference, it was really Angelo I'd seen, not Andreas as I thought. The resemblance was uncanny."

"Who was the woman he killed?" Nadia whispered in stunned horror. "Was she your wife?"

"Not yet," Gerald said grimly. "But she would have been, had she lived."

Nadia swallowed, tears forming an indigestible lump in her throat. "I'm so sorry."

He patted her shoulder. "It's all right. It's over now."

"You recognized Paros and traced him here," Lukas said after a moment. "Did you know he was a twin?"

Gerald nodded. "By that time I did. But I didn't know if they were both involved in the arms business. I asked a lot of questions, but getting any cooperation from these Epirotis is frustrating, to say the least."

"We noticed," Lukas said dryly. "And they felt they had to protect him, since he'd been there for years." His grin was quick and somewhat rueful. "Not all that plausible a cover for you, if you ask me."

Gerry grinned back. "I know, but it was the best we could do at the time. I was lucky enough, and found both Andreas and Angelo here. Although it must have been a shock for Angelo when I had the nerve to show up at his lair, so to speak, I was welcomed back as the prodigal son. But Angelo knew I wasn't there for a family reunion, and he had to do something about it. One night when I was walking back from a meeting with my men, someone ambushed me. I woke up with a knot on the side of my head, and Andreas and Angelo fighting over my body up by that cave near the quarry. Angelo wanted to kill me to keep their secret, but Andreas objected, even though he was in the business just as deeply as his brother. They fought and Andreas was shot. I managed to get up and run. Halias shot at me but only winged my arm. I hid out for a couple of days, but I kept track of what was happening in the village through an old woman."

"The old woman who took me to the cave and gave me your notebook," Nadia exclaimed. She frowned. "But Paros said she was working for him."

"She pretended to be. Even though she didn't approve of what he was doing, she was too scared to openly defy him. Until recently, when Angelo started his preparations for leaving, she cleaned his house. She's some kind of a relative, our cousin or great-aunt or something. I haven't quite figured it out."

"She tried to warn me," Nadia said softly. "Even though I misunderstood the warning. She wasn't completely under Paros's thumb."

"Not at all," Gerald agreed. "She helped me, too. Perhaps it was her way of repairing some of Paros's atrocities. She brought me food when I was hiding out with my wounded arm. She was the one who told me that Angelo had helped to spread the story that I'd had an accident. When my men arranged the funeral, he was there, putting on a good act as the bereaved father."

"Only it was his brother he was mourning," Nadia said. "When he talked about Andreas, that was the only time he seemed to have any feelings."

Gerald was silent, and Nadia knew he was thinking of Paros's sudden and violent death. "Angelo Paros was a clever man. But not clever enough. He admitted that I'd been killed. In doing so, he played into our hands."

"But why take that risk?" Nadia said. "He could have buried Andreas anywhere and ignored the funeral, since he knew you weren't dead."

Gerry frowned thoughtfully. "That bothered me, too. Only thing I can figure is that he wanted a decent burial for Andreas. When it came down to it, Angelo did care about his brother. Maybe there is something to the theory of an affinity between twins."

"Your men reported the murder that wasn't a murder," Lukas said. "No one saw the body, so how did the detailed autopsy report come about?"

"I was in pain but not totally incapacitated," Gerry explained. "I made it down to the next village before morning, to a telephone I knew Paros had no control over, and called my Athens office. They contacted my men in the village and told them what to do. In order to start an investigation by the regular police, namely you, Lukas, they released the story that I'd been murdered, and went through the charade of the funeral."

He looked at Nadia. "I'm sorry, Nadia, but it was necessary to do it that way. I needed some time to try to get back into Paros's house to find some solid evidence against him. In the end I never got it, but the result's the same." A dangerous light flared briefly in his eyes. For an instant Gerald was no longer the brother Nadia had grown up with, but a man who was capable of murder. "Paros will never sell another gun to a repressive government again."

"So your consulting firm is only a cover," Lukas said. He remained by the door, ready to take off the moment his men arrived. Before they'd left the house, he had placed another call from Paros's den, learning that the helicopter wouldn't be able to lift off until the storm let up. Well, it had, passing off without the rain that would have been welcome. The men would soon be here.

Gerald's blue eyes, so like Nadia's, now turned cold and bleak. "Can we let that remain between the three of us?"

Nadia saw the look that passed between him and Lukas; each man was conveying his deep respect for the other's efforts toward a common goal of law and peace. Lukas nodded. "Fine by me." His gaze rested briefly on Nadia. "And I'm sure Nadia won't say anything."

Suspecting and knowing were two different things, Nadia realized. She shivered as she thought of what they had just been through, what Gerald must face regularly. He was waiting for her answer, his tension charging the brief silence. "If it's what you feel you have to do, Gerry, I have to agree to keep your secret. But you know I'll worry."

Gerald squeezed her hand. "I know you will, sis, but I promise to be careful. I'm still here, aren't I?"

"Your arm?"

He wriggled it, wincing a little. "It's okay. Just a bit stiff."

The oil lamp flickered, sending long shadows up the walls. The revelry in the streets had died down along with the wind. Nadia yawned, her mouth stretching wide before she could cover it. Lukas and Gerry both laughed.

Lukas took her hand, lifting her from her chair. "I think it's time you were in bed."

Gerry stifled a cavernous yawn of his own. "Yeah, me too. I haven't slept properly in days. Shepherds' huts may keep out the rain but the ground makes a cold, hard bed." He pushed up his sweater sleeve to look at his watch. "Doesn't look as if those guys are going to make it tonight."

"Well, they'll be here in the morning."

Lukas accompanied Nadia next door to their room. She felt a faint embarrassment, wondering what Gerry was thinking of their arrangement. He said nothing, only wishing them a quiet good-night.

But at the door Lukas, who had leaned around Nadia to turn the knob, threw up his head, listening intently. Nadia heard it too, the whirring chop of a helicopter coming closer until the sound was all around them, setting off a cacophony of barking dogs. She sighed, knowing both men would have to go out again.

Gerald, his shirt unbuttoned, stepped out of his room. "Looks like we'll get no sleep, after all." He disappeared again to pull on his shoes.

Lukas ran a gentle fingertip up Nadia's cheek, tracing the dark circles under her eyes, his own soft with regret. "Sleep, Nadia. I'll be back as soon as possible."

SHE WAS SMILING as she slept. How she knew it she wasn't sure, except that she seemed to be looking down at herself. Her dreams were pleasant, no dark clouds hovered over her anymore, and she slept deeply, warm and cozy under the blankets.

The feel of Lukas's chilled skin jarred her awake, but as she absorbed the sleek feel of his nakedness against her own body, her smile widened. She turned fluidly against him, her breasts pressed into the crisp hair of his chest, her smooth thighs entwined with his hard muscled legs.

He shivered, but she sensed by the ripple that ran over his skin that it wasn't entirely due to the cold. "Lukas," she whispered. "You're back."

"Did you doubt me?" Even though her eyes were closed, she heard the smile in his voice.

She touched his face, laying her palm against the rough stubble of his growing beard. "No, never, Lukas. I love you."

"And I love you," he said. "And Gerry gives his permission for you to marry me as soon as it can be arranged."

"What?" She sat up, the blankets falling to her waist. When she would have pulled them up, Lukas laid his hand on them.

"Leave it. I've never had the time to feast on the sight of you." The room was amber with sunrise. When he laid his palm over one small breast, she forgot about the blankets.

"You mean—" she pulled in a sharp breath as his hand began to make tantalizing, wicked circles on her skin. "You mean you still want to go through with it?"

"With what?" The contrast between his dark fingers and her white skin fascinated him. "Oh, our marriage. Of course I want to go through with it."

Trembling as his hand moved lower, she wanted to tell him to stop and let her think, but the sensations singing through her blood were too delicious. "It wasn't just something you said because we were in danger?"

The hand stilled. He looked at her, his mouth set severely although his eyes twinkled. "Nadia, what do you take me for? Did you think I was just playing around?" He flopped down, covering his face with his arm. "Nadia, I'm wounded."

Nadia laughed; she couldn't help it. Gerry alive. Lukas safe. Lukas loving her. Wanting to marry her. She was suddenly aloft on a bubble of joy. She punched him playfully in the shoulder, draping her body over his, feeling a smug satisfaction as she felt the hard silky evidence of his arousal. "I'll wound you for good if you don't stop acting like a martyr."

He turned his head toward her, his expression becoming earnest. "Will you be happy here in Greece?" She couldn't know what it cost him to ask the question, but he didn't want her decision to be based on euphoria. Marriage to him would mean a major alteration in her life-style. She had to consider it seriously. "What about your work?"

Nadia tilted her head to one side. "I've found out in the past few days that there are other important things, like the certainty that we'll be alive tomorrow. I'll miss my family, though." She brightened. "But I think knowing your mother will make up for it."

Chuckling, his worries draining away, Lukas hugged her closer. "I'll bet she won't even be surprised. She'll say she guessed all the time how it would be with us." He paused. "As for your work, there are ad agencies in Athens. I'm sure some of them would welcome new blood. And we'll visit your family. I'm not exactly destitute, you know."

Nadia smiled happily. The details would have to be worked out, but in the meantime the heat engendered by Lukas's nearness was overriding logical thoughts.

She leaned over and kissed him softly, her tongue flicking at his mouth until he opened it, drawing her into his fire. "Yes, Lukas, I'll marry you. But you're not going to have everything your way. I've no intention of being a submissive wife who walks three paces behind her husband."

Lukas kissed her deeply, tenderly, his hand moving down to her hip and drawing her into the curve of his body. "I wouldn't expect you to be any other way than how you are, my proud Amazon. We'll talk about the arrangements, and we'll compromise."

The technicalities taken care of, they began to love in earnest.

Harlequin Temptation dares to be different!

Once in a while, we Temptation editors spot a romance that's truly innovative. To make sure *you* don't miss any one of these outstanding selections, we'll mark them for you.

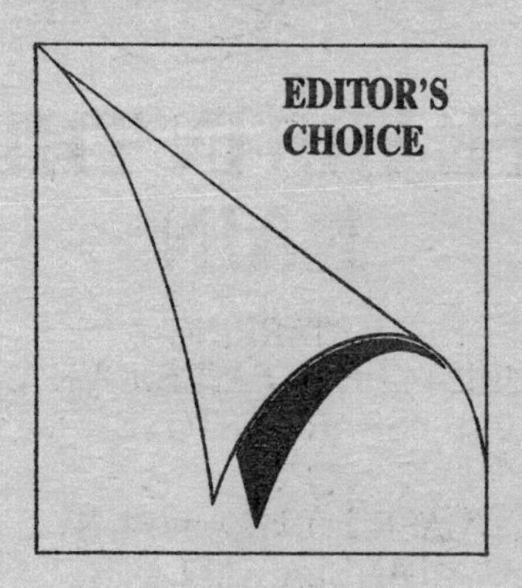

When the "Editors' Choice" fold-back appears on a Temptation cover, you'll know we've found that extra-special page-turner!

THE *Temptation* EDITORS

Spot-1B